THE Misfortune OF Lady Lucianna

THE UNDAUNTED DEBUTANTES
Book 2

CHRISTINA McKNIGHT

La Loma Elite Publishing

Christina@christinamcknight.com

PRAISE FOR CHRISTINA MCKNIGHT'S NOVELS

THE THIEF STEALS HER EARL

"When I started reading this book I could not put it down...it caused another book-hangover for me. I wanted to see how things would go when the truth of Judith came out and how Simon was going to handle it...loved it."-*Sissy's Book Review*

"Jude and Cart's story is such a delight! So refreshing to see the hero shy, socially awkward and not super wealthy. I love it...This was definitely one of the best books I've read this summer." -*Reviews from a Thrifty Mom*

FORGOTTEN NO MORE

"This author has made me love historical romance again."
-*TwinsieTalk Book Reviews*

HIDDEN NO MORE

"The storyline was really good, the writing was great. So smooth and engaging, I was able to zip right through the story, it flowed so well. I love finding new to me authors and with this wonderfully written story by Ms. McKnight I've found a new historical romance author."-*Bound by Books*

CHRISTMAS EVER MORE

"*Christmas Ever More* was a wonderfully written festive novella full of hope, renewal, love, and new beginnings. If you're a fan of Christina's Lady Forsaken series, this is a must. Even if you aren't caught up, this stands well enough on its own to be a lovely addition to your holiday reading list."-*Literal Addiction*

BOOKS BY CHRISTINA MCKNIGHT

The Undaunted Debutantes Series
The Disappearance of Lady Edith
The Misfortune of Lady Lucianna
The Misadventures of Lady Ophelia

Lady Archer's Creed Series
Theodora
Georgina
Adeline – August 2017
Josephine – November 2017

Craven House Series
The Thief Steals Her Earl
The Mistress Enchants Her Marquis
The Madame Catches Her Duke – Coming Soon
The Gambler Wagers Her Baron – Coming Soon

A Lady Forsaken Series
Shunned No More
Forgotten No More
Scorned Ever More
Christmas Ever More,
Hidden No More, A Lady Forsaken

Standalone Titles
The Siege of Lady Aloria, A de Wolfe Pack Novella
A Kiss At Christmastide
For The Love Of A Widow

DEDICATION

To Theresa and Debbie

You're always there when it counts.
Thank you for believing in me and this series!

ACKNOWLEDGMENTS

There are several people I'd like to thank for staying with me through the hectic journey of writing this book.

To Marc, my amazing boyfriend—thank you for always being *you*!

To Lauren Stewart, my critique partner and best friend, you pushed me to explore new avenues of thought that I never dreamed possible. If we were in a true relationship, it would be one based on co-dependency, but in a good way. My writing would not be what it is without your comments, criticism, suggestions, and guidance.

I'd also like to thank the wonderful women who've supported me in both my writing career and life, including (but not limited to): Erica Monroe, Amanda Mariel, Debbie Haston, Angie Stanton, Theresa Baer, Ava Stone, Roxanne Stellmacher, Laura Cummings, Dawn Borbon, Suzi Parker, Jennifer Vella, Brandi Johnson, and Latisha Kahn. I know I'm forgetting people…You have all been very patient and wonderfully supportive of my eccentric ways.

A very special thank you to my editor, Chelle Olson with Literally Addicted to Detail, your skill and professionalism surpass all that I expected. Chelle Olson can be contracted by email at. literallyaddictedtodetail@yahoo.com.

Also, a special thank you to historical and developmental editor, Scott Moreland.

And to my proofreader, Anja, thank you for embarking on yet another journey with me.

Cover design by The Midnight Muse.

Wraparound cover design credit to Sweet 'N Spicy Designs.

Finally, thank *you* for supporting indie authors.

PROLOGUE

Devonshire, England
December 1813

Lady Lucianna Constantine sat beside her dearest friend, Lady Tilda Abercorn, formally Miss Tilda Guthton—at least before her morning wedding to Lord Abercorn, a duke. Luci wanted to be happy for Tilda; she longed to feel an ounce of the joy and merriment evident in her other friends—Lady Edith and Lady Ophelia—but she simply could not find the emotion within her. So, for the moment, she settled a less than genuine smile on her face and prepared to send Tilda off for her first glimpse of what a marriage bed held.

If Tilda's shoulders appeared a bit too stiff or her posture a bit too straight, none of her friends mentioned it.

"I truly must return to my chambers before His Grace suspects I have slipped out...before our marriage was so much as consummated." Tilda leapt to her feet from the lounge.

When Lady Ophelia giggled, Lucianna joined in. The sound far lighter than her normally husky chuckle. It should be Luci preparing for her wedding night, not Tilda, the mere daughter of a baronet. As the daughter of the Marquis of Camden, Luci had always thought she would make a match long before Tilda. Or even Edith and Ophelia. It irked her to see her friend find a match before her father had even so much as mentioned any possible suitors for her.

Not that Luci would ever consider taking Abercorn, a man old enough to be her father, as husband; however, she'd always imagined she would be the first one to share all the delectable secrets found behind a closed bedchamber door.

The tall clock nestled between the bay windows had chimed midnight at least five minutes earlier.

"You will tell us everything on the morrow? At breakfast and not a moment later. I truly must know if everything is as I've been told." Luci suggestively raised one brow, wrapping Tilda in a tight embrace before withdrawing and taking in her appearance from head to stocking-covered toes. "You look breathtakingly innocent."

And utterly terrified.

Quite possibly ready to expire from her nervousness.

The other women liked to think Tilda possessed a backbone of fortified whalebone, but Luci knew differently. They'd been bosom friends since they could barely toddle about in their families' townhouses in Mayfair.

It was Edith's turn to console Tilda. "You are beautiful. You are smart. And today was a perfect way to start your married life. I only hope Ophelia, Luci, and I are blessed with such generous husbands."

Generous husbands? Tilda's spouse would be lucky to see another five years upon this earth. Luci hoped the man didn't pass to the hereafter, leaving his widow to care for an unruly horde of children—or worse yet, no offspring, and needing to find a new home when Abercorn's closest relative and heir came to claim his due.

"Thank you, Edith. You have always been a great friend." Tilda found compassion in Edith's arms, melting into the blond-haired English rose's hug. It was an emotion Luci struggled to offer—empathy for others.

She'd been taught from a young age that one fought for what they wanted. If they did not get what they desired, then it was because they hadn't wanted it badly enough. Or so her father, Lord Camden, had drilled into his four children's heads since they were knee-high.

Tilda pulled back, her smile wobbling. "I must hurry. It will not do for my *husband* to arrive in my room to find that I have fled."

Luci slipped her arms through Tilda's, while Ophelia retrieved her book and followed a few paces behind them. Luci knew Ophelia was there because the girl, no matter how many times she'd been scolded, did not see the need to lift her feet high enough to avoid shuffling.

"I will extinguish the candles," Edith called.

"Always the responsible one," Luci said over her shoulder with a smirk. The only thing that irritated her more than Ophelia's sluggish footsteps was Edith's sensible demeanor.

Luci pulled Tilda close as they walked toward the main staircase. "Now, Tilly, when I said I want to hear every word, I meant every detail!" she cooed. "Since you insisted on wedding first and rushing the ceremony before your first Season was even half over, you owe us."

Tilda's feet slowed, and the stare she turned on Luci was laced with concern...and doubt. "You know as well as I this match was my father's doing, not my own. I would have gladly waited until the end of the Season to announce my betrothal."

She placed a quick kiss on Tilda's cheek. "I know, I know. My father would have done the same had

Abercorn shown an interest in me." Luci gently turned Tilda toward the stairs and swatted her bum. "Now, get up there and greet your new husband properly."

"Luci!" Tilda hissed. "I must admit, I have no notion what you mean by that."

It did not irk her at all that Abercorn favored demure, reserved, soft brunette beauties over Luci's tall, slender frame and midnight-black hair falling all the way down her backside. No, Luci had no doubt she'd claim a dashingly handsome, witty lord as her husband. She could already picture the envious stares from other eligible men—and unattached ladies. Maybe a prince…

Tilda started up the stairs, hesitant at first, but Luci gave her a wink when Tilly glanced down at her, which gave the woman the confidence to dash up toward the final landing.

A shadow stepped into view at the top of the staircase, a hand grasping Tilda's arm.

Luci moved to better see who had stopped her friend. All the other guests had been in their chambers abed for several hours. Not even a servant had been seen since a footman had stoked the hearth over two hours before.

"No, I swear to it. I did not…" Tilda's whine sounded from atop of the stairs, a firm shake from her companion muting the remainder of Luci's friend's words.

A shock of greying hair over a red dressing robe came into view, the man's face coming within an inch of Tilda's as she pulled back.

"Tilly?" Luci called as her friend's foot slipped from the top stair, sending Tilda's arms swirling as her body fell backwards.

Tilda's mouth opened, a bone-deep scream escaping before her head hit the ground, returning the manor house to the silent stillness of a moment before. Then, Tilda's body thumped three times, finally settling on the polished floor at Luci's feet.

Luci stood silently for a moment, her mind racing to catch up with what she'd just witnessed.

Glancing up once more, she expected the man to hurry down the stairs to help Tilda, but all she saw was a flash of red and then…nothing. He was gone, vanished.

Her stomach turned as her mind raced to connect what she'd seen at the top of the stairs.

"Edith!" Lucianna's pulse raced, her scream high-pitched as she knelt by Tilda. "Ophelia!"

Another thump sounded on the floor.

Luci looked up to see Ophelia frozen in her place, her book splayed open at her feet, causing the final thump. Edith rushed in a step behind her.

"Luci." Edith stepped around Ophelia. "What is it—"

She stood, shaking her head gently.

"No, no, no," Edith sobbed as she hurried to Tilda. "This cannot be—"

"He did this." Luci couldn't hold back the accusation in her tone. Edith looked away from Tilda to where Luci stood. She pointed toward the top of the stairs, leaving no doubt who had been responsible for this.

Following Luci's indicated direction, Edith narrowed her eyes on the darkened landing above them, but Luci knew her friend would see no one lingering in the shadows.

Abercorn had fled.

"Whom?" Ophelia squeaked, walking forward to stand behind Edith.

"That is not important at this moment," Edith whispered, kneeling beside Tilda, much as Luci had done a moment before. "We must wake her up, make sure she is all right and call for the duke—and a physician."

"There is no point." Luci knelt next to Edith, sweeping Tilda's hair from her face. "She is gone."

Luci held in the sob that threatened to escape. It

was imperative that she contain her emotions, at least until the magistrate was called and an accounting of the fall recorded.

Her dear friend, so nervous—yet alive—only moments before, now stared up at the ceiling, her sightless, vacant, chestnut-brown eyes forever frozen in terror.

Anger ignited within Luci, and she begged her simmering blood to cool—at least long enough for her to speak.

"They argued." Luci grasped Edith's arm as she reached forward to touch Tilda. "He was up there, and he pushed her. I swear it."

Luci was helpless to do anything as Edith took in the mangled sight of Tilda, her white nightshift tangled between her legs, and her head tilted at an odd angle.

"Wha-wha-what should we do?" Ophelia wailed.

"We will rouse the house and tell them all what the duke did!" Lucianna shot to her feet once more. "Someone must have heard the commotion."

The foyer was deserted except for Luci, Ophelia, Edith, and, of course, Tilda.

"You are correct. I heard her scream and then the thump"—Edith visibly cringed at her choice of word, and Luci wanted to comfort her—"as she fell down."

"She did *not* fall." Lucianna knew her voice reached a dangerously high pitch as she narrowed her glare on Edith; however, she was helpless to calm the rage within her. "She was *pushed*. By Abercorn!"

Luci stared between her two remaining friends, her eyes softening, begging them to believe her.

"How could this happen?" Ophelia asked, collecting her book from the ground.

"That is a question for him. You saw him, right, Ophelia?" Luci looked toward Ophelia, her loose hair cascading over her shoulder.

The color drained from the girl's face, making her pale complexion turn almost green.

"Tell her what you saw," Luci demanded. "You were standing right here."

"I—I—I was reading." Ophelia turned to Edith, her book held tightly as if it could protect her. "I swear it, Edith, I did not see anything. I was reading about Xavier and—"

"What is going on here?" Townsend, the Abercorn butler, bustled into the foyer, his hair askew as if the noise had pulled him from slumber. "Your Grace!" His eyes widened on Tilda as he rushed across the room to where she lay. His hands moved to find her wrist and settled. "No pulse. She has no pulse!"

The servant shuffled to his feet, teetering for a moment before gaining his balance after the shock of seeing his new mistress dead at the bottom of the grand staircase—on her wedding night.

"Petunia, Petunia!" Townsend shouted, his tiny feet rushing toward the kitchens. "Petunia! We must summon His Grace. Petunia, where in all that is holy are you, woman?"

Doors opened, and voices sounded above from the guests' wing as Townsend continued calling for Petunia.

In any other situation, the scene before Luci would have incited a least a slight chuckle as the butler mimicked a bird in flight. There was no humor to be found—for anyone.

"Oh, Your Grace!" Townsend said, staring toward the top of the stairs. "Please, do not look. This is not for your eyes."

The duke stepped into view at the top of the stairs. He'd likely only retreated to the shadows down the upper hall and waited for the alarm to be sounded. However, he was still garbed in his wedding day finery with a tumbler in his hand. It could not be… He'd worn a red robe only moments before. He started down the stairs, a grey lock of hair falling before his narrowed glare as he scrutinized the scene below.

As if he hadn't watched Tilda fall backwards after

pushing her.

Luci's hands balled into fists at her sides, and her face heated in rage.

The man had pushed his new bride down the stairs and had the audacity to lumber upon the scene as if he were unaware of the death his shove had caused.

Tilda deserved better. Certainly more than the devil-may-care attitude of the scoundrel she'd wed.

Luci would see the man punished, if it were the last thing she ever accomplished.

CHAPTER 1

It is hereby announced that this writer has born witness to the Marquis of Camden scandalously parading his mistress about in polite society.

As this writer can also attest, Lady Camden and Lady Lucianna were also in attendance at the soirée the marquis saw fit to escort his mistress to.

Shame on a man who does not value family over his own pleasure.
-Mayfair Confidential, London Daily Gazette

Hanover Square, London
March 1815

"PREPOSTEROUS, SENSELESS RUBBISH." Roderick Crofton, the seventh Duke of Montrose, pushed the *London Daily Gazette* away from him on the breakfast table and scowled at his now cold morning repast. "Nothing but a scandal sheet, I tell you. Get this out of my sight."

"Certainly, Your Grace." A footman hurried forward to remove the paper. "May I bring you anything else? Tea, perhaps?"

Tea? No. Roderick did not desire tea. He craved a newspaper that took an interest in reporting true and accurate facts regarding current events, not another gossip rag that took great pleasure in ruining upstanding gentlemen.

Not that Roderick personally knew the Marquis of Camden; however, the *Mayfair Confidential* had set its sharpened teeth upon *him* only two months prior.

"Your Grace?" the footman asked once more.

"No, no, Joshua." Roderick waved his hand in dismissal. "Unfortunately, you cannot provide what I need." When the servant's shoulders slumped, he continued. "However, that is no fault of yours, I assure you."

When Joshua took his place against the wall, Roderick took hold of his utensil and pushed the cold eggs about his plate. If he did not consume at least half the food, Cook would likely chase him down and demand he eat—or else. He'd never discovered what she meant by "or else," and he damn well didn't plan to. He speared a sliver of pheasant and placed it into his mouth and then chewed slowly. Perhaps it would appear he'd eaten more if he remained at the table longer. Blast it all, but he was no longer a boy in knee breeches.

He did not need a woman, no matter that she'd known him since birth, following him like a clucking chicken. If Roderick found he was not hungry, then he would not eat.

Period.

End of story.

Until Cook gained word and saw his untouched plate.

With a sigh, he scooped a mouthful of tepid porridge from his bowl and crammed it into his mouth before he could change his mind.

He supposed someone looking after his well-being was appreciated.

For all the headaches the woman caused him, he was grateful to have her.

Joshua yelped in surprise when the sound of the

front door slamming, followed by pounding footsteps, approached the Montrose townhouse dining room.

He raised his brow in question as the dining room door slammed against its hinges, revealing his stable hand, Lucian, his clothes disheveled and his cap clutched to his heaving chest. For all his bluster, he stood silently, staring at the floor, waiting for Roderick to address him. This was the same lad Roderick had gotten into trouble with in their youths for leaving tops on the upper-floor landing—causing not one, not two, but *three* maids injury. And now, he cowered before Roderick as if he would rip the stable hand limb from limb if Lucian spoke out of turn.

"Speak, Lucian," he finally commanded.

"I have news, Your Grace," he mumbled, keeping his eyes trained on the floor.

"And are you worried this news will displease me?" Roderick pushed his onyx hair from his eyes, tucking it behind his ear. He needs must make a note to have his valet trim it or procure a stronger pomatum to keep the blasted strands from falling into his face. "Out with it."

"Your Grace, I…" Lucian started again after taking a deep breath.

"Enough with formalities," Roderick said, pushing his chair back to stand.

"I think I have finally determined the source of the *Mayfair Confidential* column." He dared a glance at Roderick and seeing his pleased expression Lucian continued. "There is a woman. She's come and gone from the *Gazette* on five occasions over the last fortnight. She was there in the late-night hours, and while I have not confirmed, I suspect a new column was printed in the *London Daily Gazette* today."

"You are correct." Roderick nodded to Joshua to remove his plate of hardly touched food. "Have you ascertained the woman's identity?"

A moment of excitement hung in the air.

"No, Your Grace." Lucian shook his head. "I

wanted to make certain you approved of me looking further into the matter. I do know she does not find full-time employment at the paper, nor does she have relatives within the *Gazette*. I asked about the business, but no one was familiar with her—or they refused to comment."

"Of course, I want you to investigate further." Roderick's command thundered, and once again, standing against the wall, Joshua flinched. "This woman, whoever she may be, is responsible for destroying my life. I will see she pays for her actions." He needs must calm his anger, especially if he wanted to keep his footman from expiring from fright. "What can you tell me of this woman? Is it possible I am acquainted with her?"

Lucian pulled at his coat as if noting for the first time his ramshackle appearance. "She arrives in a fancy carriage each time, leaving it down the street. She enters the business without so much as a glance over her shoulder. This was why it took me so long to figure her out. If I were the one exposing men of the *ton*, I would be paranoid and watching my back at every turn. But this woman, her chin is always high, raven hair always perfectly groomed, and her gowns are impeccable, likely made by the finest modiste in London."

"You suspect she is of noble birth?" Why hadn't the notion crossed his mind before? Roderick had suspected the culprit to be a jealous lord, not a woman—especially not a lady of class.

"I have little doubt of it, Your Grace."

"Then you have my permission to look into the woman further; however…" This was not an entirely new venture, sleuthing. He'd been investigating random men and businesses for several years now; though it was imperative that he not draw attention to his activities. "Do not let the woman know we are on to her, or she is likely to vanish."

"Certainly, Your Grace. I will bring you

information as soon as I know anything more." Lucian bowed and turned to leave.

"And, Lucian."

"Yes, Your Grace?"

"Do bathe and get some rest before going back out."

The servant smiled, wearily. "Thank you, Your Grace."

Roderick glanced back toward the footman pressed against the far wall; he seemed unimpressed and no less anxious by the kindness Roderick had shown Lucian.

No matter, he had many important things to accomplish, far more dire than convincing a new servant he was not the beast he appeared to be despite his jet-black hair, severe jawline, and penetrating ice-blue eyes. He only knew these terms for a gentleman's appearance because Lady Daphne was always going on and on about his dashingly handsome face.

His gut twisted at the thought of the young woman, so innocent and shy. It would have been a pleasure to take her as wife and make her the Duchess of Montrose. Yet, that had been another thing stripped from him by the *Mayfair Confidential*. What his father's dastardly friends hadn't stolen from him, the person who'd published the damning column in the *London Daily Gazette* had.

He could remember every scandalous word:

It is hereby stated that this writer has born firsthand witness to the 7th Duke of Montrose, scandalously alone with a golden-haired nymph in his private opera box, all whilst betrothed to Lady Daphne.

As this writer can also attest, Lady Daphne's hair is pure night, compared to the observed doxy's crown of light. Let this article stand as proof that Lady Daphne would do well to find herself another eligible lord to take as husband.

-Mayfair Confidential, London Daily Gazette

Lady Daphne's father had decided to do just that: secure another eligible lord for her to take as husband.

Roderick had been so hell-bent on finding out the truth of his family's missing fortune, he hadn't even thought about the repercussions of being seen in public with another woman. At first, he'd pondered the idea that the *Mayfair Confidential* writer had actually done him a glorious favor. He hadn't loved Daphne. She was sweet, innocent, and beautifully angelic even with her dark locks. And with time, he had no doubt an affection would have grown between them, despite the girl's lack of passion for anything of substance.

Bloody hell. His fury over the situation returned whenever he thought of it; his pulse beating erratically, and his blood hammering through him.

There was no more Lady Daphne in his future. And with her gone, so was the dowry he'd counted on to restore at least a portion of his family's coffers. Admittedly, it was much less than he needed to secure the Montrose line and keep it from ruin, but it would have bought him enough time to find the men responsible for swindling his father out of every coin not nailed down.

He should be donning riding garb and Hessians for an afternoon at Hyde or Regent's Park to socialize and search for a new bride. If he had half the sense he claimed to have, Roderick would be doing just that. Unfortunately, he'd inherited more than just his midnight looks from his father. Apparently, he'd also gained his lack of wisdom.

The time would come to begin his search anew for a wife, but that wasn't now. Perhaps he'd look through the few invitations that had arrived over the last few days and select a few social gatherings to attend. Maybe a ball or a recital.

At the moment, Roderick needed something to ease his fury and cool his heated blood. That was something a ride in Hyde Park could not do.

However, he knew the exact place it was acceptable to thrash another—and it was called sport.

CHAPTER 2

LUCIANNA WANTED NOTHING more than to strike down the man before her; however, he was not the cause of her rage. Nevertheless, he would do for now. She gracefully stepped back as her opponent lunged at her. Behind her mask, she grinned as the man's foil thrust into empty air.

Recovering quickly, he returned to the *en garde* position and awaited her next move.

She took a deep breath, though it did nothing to calm the raging current within her.

The nerve of her father, bringing his mistress to a ball when he knew bloody well his wife and daughter would be in attendance. It was the height of embarrassment. What galled her further was the way her mother, Lady Camden—a pillar of London society— had shrugged and moved on to the refreshment table as if there were nothing she could do about it. As if she weren't utterly mortified by her husband's scandalous actions. At one time, her mother, Eloise Constantine, had been the envy of every woman at the ball. The rare, dark beauty every woman wanted to be and every man wanted to bed. But nearly twenty-two years with Luci's father had broken something in the woman.

Not broken…utterly obliterated.

With time, her dark locks had lost their luster and finally given over to grey, her shoulders were not as straight as they'd once been, and her friends had, one by one, distanced themselves from the marchioness.

Did they think Luci's father's rakehell ways would rub off on their own dear husbands?

Luci didn't doubt for a second her father would corrupt any man that gave him a speck of devotion. She'd spent years outraged over her mother's situation, but what could a mere child do to change anything, especially when Lady Camden appeared unconcerned with her position.

Luci held her foil out in a point-in-line manner. She tired of this match.

She could have bested her opponent in her sleep.

This would force him to defend himself by enforcing a beat, a tap to her blade to either initiate an attack or provoke a reaction from her.

There was nothing more she wanted than for her opponent to force her to react.

The match had been one of parry and counter thus far. No grand moves, no unexpected *flèche*, and certainly no feint.

Luci had come to Bentley's to work off her aggression and anger from the night before; instead, she felt as if she were matched with an amateur. After returning home, she'd hastily hurried to Ophelia's townhouse and instructed her friend to write the *Mayfair Confidential* column about her father. Lady Ophelia had done her best to persuade Luci not to write such damning things about her own family—that it could ultimately harm her own reputation. Luci didn't care. She was beyond giving a whit about her future prospects. Not to mention, she'd failed to make the acquaintance of a man worthy of her love, let alone her respect.

Lord Torrington, Lady Edith's betrothed, was the exception, though she was loath to admit the fact aloud.

The man had an overinflated, arrogant notion of his own self-worth as it was, and there was absolutely no way Luci would give the man more fodder with which to build himself on.

Regardless, it was her father whom Luci truly wanted at the tip of her foil.

Comical since fencing was the one thing her father had taught his eldest daughter. The only thing of worth the marquis had passed on to her as yet. The memories flooded her; not many fond ones surfaced, overshadowed by hours spent at the tip of her father's foil as she learned harsh lesson after harsh lesson.

Never had her father taken compassion on her, even during her first years of learning.

Her opponent hadn't made the decision to attack or force her to attack.

Taking one step forward, she thrust the tip of her foil in his direction—a challenge, of sorts.

Their masks made it impossible for her to tell what the man felt—either reluctance or renewed confidence. And, she knew, neither did he suspect his opponent was a woman. Which was for the best. Luci didn't desire for anyone to go easy on her because she was female—they were all sportsmen at Bentley's. Her tall stature and wide shoulders were only embellished by her outfitting.

Her opponent lowered his foil tip to the ground at his side, admitting defeat.

Bollocks.

It appeared she was not to gain the vigorous match she'd desired.

A part of her longed to place her tip at the man's heart, forcing him to defend himself; however, unsportsmanlike conduct would have her membership revoked. It was something she'd never jeopardize.

Luci rolled her neck from side to side, dispelling the stiffness that came with hours on the strip. No doubt also partly due to her forgoing sleep the previous night to make certain the column reached the *London*

Daily Gazette in time to be printed in this morning's post.

No matter that Edith was distracted by Lord Torrington and their coming betrothal ball, and Ophelia would rather have her nose in a book, Lucianna was still determined to fulfill their promise from the night of Tilda's death. She would expose any scoundrels for their misdeeds, and her own father was not beyond her vengeance. The man she longed to rip apart before all of society—Lord Abercorn—remained just out of reach. But she was certain he could not escape for long.

Her opponent bowed stiffly and departed the strip.

Luci was capable of biding her time. Abercorn would misstep eventually—she was certain of it—and Lucianna would be there to take him down. Permanently.

Turning, she surveyed the room for her next match partner; however, the pickings were slim this early in the day. Many men—the lords who could afford the dues at Bentley's—were barely breaking their fast at this hour.

"Are you prepared to take on a skilled opponent, my lord?" A man stepped from the shadows created by the rack holding spare foils and other gear. He was tall, even by her standards, with massively broad shoulders. Thankfully, a man's sheer size normally spoke of their less than agile abilities. His mask in place and his foil at the ready, he didn't wait for her response but joined her on the strip. "*En garde.*"

His impertinent manners were overlooked when she noted his expert stance and strong hold.

This was the opponent she'd been waiting for— and his disregard for proper etiquette only fueled her ire.

Exhilaration hummed through her, but she focused her entire being on the match to come—the correct footwork, the perfect hold on her foil, and, lastly, the appropriate set of moves to gain the win.

Luci lowered her chin and immediately advanced,

her need to take control of the match overpowering her common sense to bide her time and assess the fencer's skill set.

He expertly parried her action.

She'd learned years before to always knot her waist-length hair tightly and securely under her mask—or face the consequences. Namely, male opponents treating her like a weak female as opposed to the accomplished sportswoman she was. Thirteen years of daily fencing lessons would turn any girl into a fierce competitor—either that, or break their spirit. Luci allowed no one and nothing to bring her down, especially not her father's relentless need to best his children at the one sport he could muster any talent for.

Very advantageous for her father that business was not considered a sport.

Regrettably for Lord Camden, Luci, his eldest child, had mastered the art of fencing by the young age of fourteen.

After a year of lost matches, Luci's father refused to spar with her and had instead purchased her membership at Bentley's.

The buzz of her opponent's foil sounded close to her ear as he advanced, forcing her to back step or risk injury. His skill was something she hadn't witnessed at Bentley's before, nor did she recognize the man's voice.

She needs must keep her head on the match—not on her father's scandalous activities or their rough past as father and daughter.

And most positively not on attempting to identify her opponent.

Concentrating on the set of her feet, she knew a match could be won—or just as easily lost—because of footwork.

Luci cross-stepped, bringing her farther from his dominant hand, but he was too quick and anticipated the novice move, bringing his foil around. She was forced into a *passata sotto*, twisting and lowering herself under his weapon and holding herself balanced with her free hand upon the ground. She moved to attempt an upward thrust with her own foil, hoping to catch her opponent off guard; however, he'd deftly accomplished a riposte and outmaneuvered her point.

He was a worthy opponent, indeed.

Recovering quickly, she prepared her next move.

It had been many months since she'd located a fencer with half the skill she possessed.

But his retreat gave her ample time to reset and contemplate her next move.

She must think two steps ahead. She quickly advanced with a straight extension, knowing any decent opponent would parry, and she'd be forced to disengage, twisting her foil. But she expertly changed tactic to an expulsion, successfully opening the man's defenses. Before he knew her course, the tip of her foil was aimed directly at his heart. Victory surged through her. The thrashing of her heart as she allowed herself several deep inhales and exhales, echoed through her head.

She expected him to enact some practiced maneuver, removing the tip from his breast, but instead, he chuckled and flipped up his mask.

Luci was not fool enough to think her opponent had no other moves planned, and she kept her tip trained on him until he lowered his foil in surrender.

She had the oddest sense it was not a move of defeat but one of promise for another time.

She narrowed her glare on him, her irritation only growing. The man had not shown her his true capabilities on the strip, but had only seen the match as spirited fun. Luci did not have the same opinion, and she wished to slash her foil before his face to remove his smug grin.

"To whom do I owe the honor of my first loss in too many years to count?" he asked, his blue eyes sparkling. A nagging sensation of recognition filled her.

He completely removed his mask, revealing hair of the darkest black—so deep, Luci thought she saw hints of blue. It was a shade darker than hers, which Luci hadn't thought possible. His locks were midnight obsidian, while his eyes were as clear as the blue sea. "Come now, lad. You are certainly skilled and deserve to be commended."

She studied the set of his jaw, his extreme height, and commanding presence. Where had she seen the man before?

Her rule was to never, ever remove her mask while on the strip. Never reveal that she was a lady. And, under no circumstances, allow any man the opportunity to go soft on her during a match based on her femininity. She entered Bentley's prepared to fence and only removed her mask when she'd once again gained the safety of her carriage. Bentley's proprietor had never betrayed her confidence, which she suspected had more to do with her father's money as opposed to any loyalty to Luci.

However, a piece of her needed to show the arrogant man that a mere woman had bested him. Longed to show the haughty lord that no matter his superior demeanor, he was no competition for her…

Slowly, she pushed her mask up and completely off her head. A tumble of dark waves cascaded down her back and over her shoulders. Luci flipped her head as she tucked her gear under her arm, sending her long tresses out of her face.

His mouth gaped, and his brow rose in question.

Luci knew well the sight he beheld: ebony waves of hair, piercing, intense green eyes, and sun-kissed skin. She was tall in stature, and every inch the lady many women envied—just as every woman had envied Luci's mother in her day. This man now took in her regal stare and supple curves in her masculine garb—though it was tailored to hug every inch of her body.

From the lust in his open stare, he had noted every

womanly curve he'd only moments ago attributed to the form of a young lad.

It was Luci's turn to smirk.

And smile she did. "You may show proper honor to my skill by collecting your senses and closing your gaping mouth, or I will think you find it offensive to be bested by a woman." Luci outright grinned, pride swelling inside her to finally have the nerve to expose her face to one of her defeated opponents. "You may issue your accolades whenever you are ready…and it is my lady, not my lord."

He stalled for a moment before speaking. "I must say, the only thing to overshadow your skill with a foil is your beauty, *my lady*." He bowed slowly, his eyes traveling the length of her as he did.

Luci could feel the heat of his stare as it took in her form for the second time.

She'd never had occasion to overthink her preferred fencing attire, that of her male counterparts, to be scandalous or revealing in any overt manner. But his intense scrutiny scorched her from her face, down to her toes, and back up again. It was not hard to imagine her face blossoming with heat, as well. She would give him due credit for his eyes only lingered at her bosom—barely noticeable under her tightly bound cloth wrap—a brief moment before returning to her face.

However, his inspection gave her time to look closer at him. He was as tall as she'd suspected, and just as broad, his fencing attire not adding to his size as hers did. His hair hung nearly to his shoulders in a way far less gentlemanly than was preferred in London's premier ballrooms. But it was his eyes that attracted her notice most. Their blue depths held something she couldn't quite place her finger on. Hurt? Anger? Betrayal?

What could this lordly arrogant man know of these things?

His examination of her person sent a shiver down

Luci's spine, and all her defenses, bred through years of dealing with her father and competing in fencing, jumped into action. She should pivot, turn and flee Bentley's immediately; instead, she asked, "Your name, kind lord? I wish to add it to my extensive list of conquests."

She would never allow him to know of his appeal. When a man was given the upper hand in any situation, it was Luci's experience that they used it to exploit others and gain exactly what they searched for. Though there couldn't be anything the dark-haired lord sought from Luci. Only a moment before, he'd had no notion whom he sparred against, let alone that she was the eldest daughter of the Marquis of Camden.

His grin only widened when he snorted with laughter.

Was the man overly familiar with such blasé commentary from the women he associated with?

Luci was in the presence of a rogue—a taker of the innocent, a philanderer with no moral compass, a charlatan in lord's attire. The set of his crooked, self-assured grin, and his open appraisal of her was something Luci had witnessed on at least a dozen occasions.

She knew the type well, had lived under the roof of such a man her entire life—and called him *father*.

"What is so amusing?" she asked when he continued to grin at her after this laughter had ceased— likely due to her penetrating stare and uplifted chin. "Do you think it luck that handed me the win today?"

"Oh, certainly not, my lady." He moved and set his mask and foil on the bench against the far wall and then proceeded to remove his gloves, his back to her. "For a lad, your skill was at an expert level, but for a woman?" He shook his head and turned back to face her. "It was complete mastery—a practiced prowess many men never achieve in all their years at the sport."

Her face flushed—from the compliment or the

overt use of the word *prowess*, she was uncertain. "I am overjoyed to see that we are in agreement of my skill, and furthermore, your need to study the sport more thoroughly before our next match." She rocked back on her heels, not attempting to hide her smugness over her victory and her mastery of their back and forth banter.

As he paced back toward her, he tapped his bottom lip with his forefinger. "And what, my lady, makes you think I would agree to another match only to be bested soundly once more?"

It was Luci's turn to laugh. Her deep chuckle filled the room, empty except for her and the jet-black-haired man before her. His shoulders stiffened when she expressed her own merriment with the situation. "Are you saying you would turn down another round of sparring?"

"I said nothing of the sort; however"—he halted several feet from her—"I am not in the routine of agreeing to things if there is no chance of them working in my favor.

"Well, I never offer if I do not know I will win." Luci tilted her chin up a notch.

"Your name, my lady?" he requested again, his stare returning to its former intensity and never leaving hers. He was not appreciating her womanly curves nor waxing poetic prose about her silky hair and vibrant green eyes. It appeared he truly wished to learn her given name. "My lady?" His brow arched in question.

She should not give her name, but there was something about the man that pulled the words from her. It could be his sincerity, his forthright nature, or possibly his confidence in being bested by a woman at a predominately male sport. "Lady Lucianna Constantine, my lord."

"Your Grace."

"Pardon?"

"It is *Your Grace*." His smirk returned as he seemed to go from intense to playful with each breath he took.

"The Duke of Montrose, but you may call me Roderick—you have bested me with a foil, after all."

All thoughts of her own coy nature disappeared quickly with the one damning name.

As she'd suspected, he was a rogue, a rakehell, and a debauched man.

And the very first lord she'd taken down with the *Mayfair Confidential.*

The exhilaration from her victory on the strip dissipated.

CHAPTER 3

RODERICK WHISTLED AS he stepped through his townhouse door just as the sun was setting on the day. The shock on his butler's face was evident; however, he was still wholly focused on the nimble beauty that was Lady Lucianna. He'd attended Bentley's for several years now and had never crossed paths with the woman. Or had he? Would he have known a woman resided under her fencing attire?

Their time together had ended quickly when he'd given his name, as she'd no doubt recognized him from the scandal two months prior, when he'd been falsely accused of being unfaithful to Lady Daphne—his betrothed. But the gossip sheets had gotten it all wrong.

Unfortunately, Lady Lucianna hadn't given him the time to explain anything. Bloody hell, he wasn't even certain that was the reason her entire demeanor had changed and she had hurried off.

Blast it all, but he couldn't resist thinking of her tightly clad legs that had seemingly gone on forever. No skirting with petticoats and underpinnings to hide the muscular curves of her calves or the toned expanses of her thighs.

He shook the image of said thighs wrapped tightly around his waist from his mind as he handed his overcoat to the waiting servant.

He'd thought of her well-trimmed, slender frame—while she'd been plotting her escape.

"Your Grace, Lucian awaits you in your study." The butler dipped his head and hurried off.

Lucian had returned already?

Roderick had expected the servant to rest and return to the *Gazette* on the morrow, or by earliest that night.

"Inform him I will see him now." His words echoed in the empty foyer; his butler having departed for parts unknown. "I suppose I can inform him myself," he mumbled, starting down the hall toward his study.

The man's news could only serve to further brighten his day after so many months—nay, years—of desolation caused by his father's reckless investments, and then that bloody column.

The tides were turning.

They had to at some point, and the closer he came to the study the more hope surged.

Roderick could practically feel the weight being lifted from his shoulders. Not that knowing the identity of the *Mayfair Confidential* authoress would solve all his financial—and social—problems; however, it would be a start; a way to gain some semblance of control over his life, which had been spinning endlessly out of his control for some time.

He strode into the study, pushing the door closed behind him, and smiled at Lucian. "I hadn't expected to see you for a few days."

Lucian stood from his chair before Roderick's desk, wringing his hat in his hands once again. Roderick needs must remember to explain to the servant that the nervous gesture did not invoke a sense of confidence. If Lucian ever expected to gain employment with Bow Street as a runner, he need hold his head high and meet every man's eye, regardless of their station and status.

"I have news, Your Grace." Lucian's head dipped.

"You have secured her identity?" Roderick still found it hard to believe a woman—a gently bred lady at that—was behind the atrocious column that had stolen his future. Though, after his morning at Bentley's, Roderick now understood women sometimes exceeded what men thought of them. Their roles not so specifically fitting into the neat square society and generations of teaching had created for them.

"I have, Your Grace." For the first time since agreeing to take on the assignment, Lucian smiled. He'd successfully completed a task Roderick had assigned to him. "The authoress is none other than Lady Lucianna Constantine, eldest daughter of the Marquis of Camden."

Roderick felt like he'd been punched in the gut...and pushed off a cliff. The name dispelled any light that had begun to peek through the gloomy haze that had settled over his life.

"Are you certain?" He half expected the servant to laugh, slap him on the back, and jest about the look of horror that'd crossed Roderick's face before informing him that he'd seen him leave Bentley's earlier in the day.

However, that was not to happen.

"Yes." Lucian nodded severely, completely sober. "I sketched the crest on the carriage door a few nights ago and I finally found another servant—in Lord Esquire's employ—who knew the family name. It did not take long to locate the Camden townhouse in Mayfair, and I saw Lady Lucianna return home at midday."

The irony of her townhouse location and the name of her column was not lost on Roderick.

"Does the marquis have other children, perchance?"

"Yes, Your Grace, but I have been told they are all still in the schoolroom."

She'd known all along whom he was at Bentley's.

Her coy, playful manner was all a jest at his expense. The entire time, he'd been mooning over her skill and beauty, she'd known full well he was the man she'd ruined with her fallacious ramblings in the *London Daily Gazette*.

Breathing deeply, Roderick attempted to suppress his anger.

He'd enjoyed almost an entire day without the need to slam his fist into a wall or throw a door closed until it fell from its hinges.

He'd been a fool to think any weight had been lifted or that his days living under a cloud of scandal were to be dispelled so easily. All so simply vanquished by learning the identity of one alluring, captivating, and utterly enchanting beauty.

The back of his throat soured at the thought.

The woman would pay for the havoc she'd caused in his life.

"Where is she now?" he asked.

"I left her at the Earl of Shaftesbury's townhouse," Lucian said. "She arrived in a fine blue gown with her mother. I suspect they will be there until the end of the evening. I asked a coachman, and he said they were gathering for Lady Edith Pelton and Lord Torrington's betrothal ball."

"Wonderful," Roderick seethed. She'd ruined his life, made a fool of him at Bentley's, and now she planned to spend her evening twirling about a dance floor and drinking spiced sherry? Oh, no. "You are dismissed."

"Thank you, Your Grace." The servant turned on his heels and stalked from the room, a rare moment of confidence infusing his long stride.

Unfortunately, every ounce of the confidence born and bred into Roderick as the heir to a Dukedom had fled the moment Lucian had uttered Lady Lucianna's name. He'd scrutinized her with longing not long before—had thought of future matches between them.

All impossible now as he'd misjudged her interested in him.

Roderick would not cower. He would not hide his head in shame. He had done nothing wrong by escorting the widow Cavendish to the opera. They were friends—the former Duke of Montrose being close to the widow's late husband.

Blast it all, but he was a duke…and no mere slip of a debutante would be the cause of his thorough ruination.

Not without severe consequences.

He'd been debating whether to accept an invitation to a soirée or garden party that very morning. It was long past time Roderick donned his ballroom finery—and attended a betrothal celebration…with or without a proper invitation.

CHAPTER 4

THE NIGHT WAS purely magical. Everything that Edith and Triston—Lord Torrington—deserved in their betrothal ball. The *ton* had turned out in droves, not an invite turned down as they all clamored to the Earl of Shaftesbury's Mayfair townhouse to gain a look at the new couple. Their love story, or at least what society had been told, started when Lord Torrington had dashingly rescued Edith, Luci, and Ophelia from a carriage accident outside of London.

Thankfully, no one had inquired as to why the ladies had ventured into the English countryside unchaperoned, or how their parents had not discovered they'd been missing an entire day, which was advantageous for the trio because there had been no carriage accident. However, Lord Torrington had rescued Edith from the clutches of his evil stepmother, who'd kidnapped her from the London streets and whisked her off to the seaside cliffs of Southend.

All had been set to rights since her rescue the month before, and now, Luci adored Torrington as much as Edith and Ophelia did. He was a man above all men, and one not tarnished by scandalous misdeeds—all too common in Englishmen.

He was perfect for Lady Edith.

"It is allowed for one to be envious of a friend so long as it does not cross the line to jealousy," Luci recited quietly as she watched Edith, held securely to Triston's side as they greeted guests and walked the perimeter of the ballroom.

Everything was perfect.

As Luci knew the couple's future would be.

"I am surprised you are not dancing this set," Ophelia said, handing Luci a flute of champagne as she turned to examine their dear friend and her betrothed greeting yet another couple who'd joined the ball.

Luci stifled another yawn. "I am exhausted. After staying up all night to deliver and make certain the column was posted, and then my morning at Bentley's, followed by helping Edith prepare for this grand soirée, I am falling asleep on my feet."

Ophelia fanned her face and took a sip from her champagne. "Mayhap, if you'd listened to me and not been in such an uproar over your father's actions and your need to harm him, you would have gotten at least a bit of sleep last night."

"And we both know how I excel at taking orders from others." Luci glanced at Ophelia out of the corner of her eye. The woman with her auburn hair, fair skin, and pale blue eyes was as exotic as Luci was, but in a wholly different and more innocent manner. Luci was all dark with her long, black hair, startlingly green, catlike eyes, and height as tall as most men. Ophelia was pure light—if she would ever come out of her shell and allow herself to shine.

"Oh, look!" the woman exclaimed, pulling Luci's attention back to the crowded room in time to see her father depart the card room with none other than Lord Abercorn. "What is your father doing with that vile man?"

"A better question is: why was Abercorn issued an invitation at all?" Luci seethed.

"Come now, Luci," Ophelia chastised. "Abercorn

is Lord Torrington's neighbor. And no one would want to offend the man, lest he spread rumors about what truly happened when Edith was taken. And, as far as Edith is concerned, she thinks it best to keep her friends close and our enemies closer."

"Very true." Luci narrowed her gaze on the men, wishing her look would set the pair ablaze. While her father hadn't killed anyone—that she knew of—the Marquis of Camden and the Duke of Abercorn were identical in many ways. "When he drops his guard, we need be close and ready to expose him. The man will not get away with Tilda's death, I assure you of that. He should have been hauled off by the magistrate the very night it occurred."

"You know I agree with you, but there just was not enough proof that he pushed her, Luci." Ophelia snapped her fan shut and turned her stare back to Edith and Lord Torrington, who were now moving in their direction.

Ophelia could refuse to discuss the topic all she desired, but Luci knew full well what she'd seen. Abercorn and Tilda had argued, he'd shaken her, and then Tilly was plummeting to the ground floor at Luci's feet. How Abercorn had changed from his red dressing robe back to his formal attire, Luci wasn't certain, but she knew he had been the one to kill Tilda.

If only her two friends had spoken up that night, aligned with Luci and pointed the finger at Abercorn, none of this would be happening now. Then again, the *Mayfair Confidential* column would not exist, Edith would not have met Torrington, and Luci would not have had to run from her fencing club after learning the name of her opponent that morning.

So many things would be different. Maybe the trio of them would have completed their first Season and found loving, honorable husbands, instead of observing the appropriate mourning period for Tilda.

Unfortunately, none of them would know how

things could have turned out.

"You are scowling, Luci," Ophelia hissed, nudging her elbow into Luci's hip. "And people are starting to notice."

"Let them stare. The girl who cried wolf," Luci mimicked the name she'd heard society call her behind her back; however, she attempted at least a look of passivity as opposed to an outright frown. "I will not be happy until Abercorn has been punished."

"Be that as it may, tonight is not that night." Ophelia drained her glass before continuing. "Tonight is about celebrating Edith and Lord Torrington and their upcoming nuptials. Do you think you can find an agreeable demeanor for at least another couple of hours?"

"For Edith, I can." But that did not mean she could stop the fury she felt over her father and Abercorn from heating her insides.

"Very good. Now, look, a new guest is arriving." Ophelia stood on tiptoes as the butler announced the new guest. "I do hope it is Lady Prudence and Lady Chastity. They are great fun."

Lord Torrington's younger sisters were acceptable as debutantes went. They weren't vain or featherbrained, which were things Luci could not tolerate in a friend. However, Luci hadn't taken the time to truly get to know the women. It would behoove her to try. After Edith's wedding, the pair was likely to be underfoot a lot.

"...the Duke of Montrose."

Luci's eyes snapped to the ballroom entrance as Montrose took the first step into the room.

Her heart stopped for what seemed like several long moments as he searched the crowd. He was looking for someone—and it was highly likely it was she.

Had he discovered her to be the woman who'd exposed him? Certainly not. No one knew who was behind the *Mayfair Confidential* column in the *London Daily Gazette*. They'd been extremely careful with the entire activity. They'd only delivered under cover of night—Luci having taken over the duty of bringing Ophelia's final column to the *Gazette* building while Edith was occupied with preparing for her wedding.

Blessedly, Edith and Torrington arrived at that moment, and Luci slipped her arm through Ophelia's and motioned for the couple to follow them.

The terrace doors lay open and only a short distance away. Luci practically dragged Ophelia toward them, skirting lords and ladies as they went until the fresh night air surrounded them.

Luci turned, keeping Ophelia at her side and hoping Lord Torrington would block her from view.

"Did you hear who arrived only moments ago?" Ophelia said a bit enthusiastically for Luci's liking.

"Who?" Edith made to look back into the ballroom to search the crowd.

"Do not look," Luci hissed. "He is coming this way, and he is certainly angry!"

"I can only imagine what trouble you ladies are embroiled in now." Triston scrutinized Luci and Ophelia, seeming to forget that his own bride-to-be was just as entangled as they were. "However, this night belongs to Edith and me, and I will not have anything distracting me from her beauty and our future happiness."

With a grand flourish, he twirled Edith back toward the ballroom, his hand firmly at the small of her back.

The action gave Luci a clear line of sight into the space.

Which meant Montrose was also able to see her. And he was stalking her way, unaware of the people who leapt out of his way or the people who stared in his wake.

"Ophelia," Luci whispered, unable to remove her eyes from the man. "I need you to cause a distraction."

"Me?" she squeaked. "I do not—"

"Yes, you. Only long enough for me to hide in the garden."

"But, why ever would you—"

"There is no time." Luci pushed the auburn-haired woman toward the terrace door. "I will keep out of sight by the cherub fountain. Come and get me when he leaves."

Luci didn't wait to see if Ophelia did as she demanded. She grasped the skirts of her midnight-blue gown and hurried down the stairs into the Shaftesbury's gardens. The paths were unlit, keeping other guests from exploring the natural wonders, but Luci knew the area well. She and her friends had enjoyed spring and summer picnics between the many rose bushes and gardenia plants during their youths. They'd learned to play lawn bowls and the game of graces on the expanse of green bordering the gardens.

Even by moonlight, Luci had no trouble finding her way.

The moment she stepped onto the lawn-covered path leading around the statue she sought, her delicate, black slippers soaked up the evening dew. Her footwear was ruined, and her stockings would likely be stained beyond repair. It mattered naught.

Luci ducked behind the fountain, a towering monstrosity of curiously entwined, nude cherubs. They'd inspected the piece at great length in their childhoods, Edith being the first to notice that two of the three angels were not fashioned properly. They had an extra *attachment* below their extended bellies.

They dared to question Lady Shaftesbury about the oddity only once—the woman's face flaring scarlet before declaring the question was not fit for young girls to ask.

Kneeling behind the statue, Luci no longer cared about ruining her gown. She needs must remain out of sight and undiscovered. Montrose must certainly be upset about her besting him with a foil. There was no other reason he could be here. Could there? Edith would never invite a man they'd exposed; which left only the possibility that he'd stormed into Lady Edith betrothal ball without invitation—specifically to find Luci.

CHAPTER 5

RODERICK HAD GAINED entrance to Lord Torrington and Lady Edith's betrothal ball without incident. No household in the *beau monde* would dare turn away a duke, invited or not. He hadn't bothered to stop long enough to remove his jacket and hand it to the footman. His purpose and course were clear: he would find Lady Lucianna and make her admit her part in his ruination.

Then what?

The woman was not capable of setting things to rights; she could not fix his broken relationship with Lady Daphne, nor could she restore his family's missing fortune. Lady Lucianna was not in possession of the information Roderick sought.

Nevertheless, he was certain he would find peace with this current situation once he confronted the woman responsible.

And she had to be in this very room.

Sure enough, Roderick spotted Lady Lucianna on the terrace of the Shaftesbury's townhouse. The terror in her widened stare told him she knew exactly why he had come. He continued across the ballroom. If he cut directly through the dancing couples, he paid no mind. His sights were set on one thing…and one thing only.

Vengeance.

In the form of Lady Lucianna.

A couple reentered the ballroom and hurried past him, but he kept his narrowed glare on the object of his ire.

A wisp of pale green, followed by the face of an auburn-haired woman moved to block his path—and his sight—as she stood on her tiptoes just inside the double doors, wavering from side to side.

"Excuse me, miss." Roderick made to step around the woman, but she stepped in the same direction, blocking him once more.

The slip of a woman giggled—giggled!—but finally stepped around Roderick with a simple word of apology. "Do beg my pardon."

He nodded curtly to her, but she'd already flitted farther into the room.

Leaving Roderick free to pursue Lady Lucianna on the terrace.

He stalked through the open doors, his narrowed glare sweeping across the outdoor patio and back again.

His hands clenched at this sides as he inspected the two couples on the terrace. Neither included Lucianna.

"Where in the bloody hell has she made off to?" he muttered, gaining a puzzled glance from one of the couples.

There was no way to escape but back into the ballroom—or down the steps into the unlit gardens below. The collection of shrubs, hedges, rose bushes, various flower blossoms, arches, benches, and statues seem to go on forever from his vantage point, at least until the night cast everything into utter darkness.

She was down there, Roderick could sense it.

It was possible she watched him even now; getting a laugh that she'd outmaneuvered him once more. His irritation swelled to the point of boiling over at her avoidance of a situation she'd caused.

She may have had the last say earlier in the day, but

they were on even ground now. She'd known who he was at Bentley's. And now, he knew who she was.

Tonight, *he* was determined to have the final word.

Roderick shoved his hands into the pockets of his evening coat, thankful he hadn't stopped to hand it over to the footman, and started down the steps into the cold, dark gardens below.

The second his Hessians hit the soft, damp grass of the nearest path, he was also glad he'd forgone his ballroom shoes. It was enough that his valet would give him hell for the disrepair his boots would surely be in by the end of his excursion to find Lady Lucianna.

Nevertheless, he pushed onward. The dew from a blue blossom clung to his sleeve, and he brushed it away.

Each path he ventured down was empty.

Each hidden seating area was vacant.

Finally, the narrow path he'd selected opened into a large, circular area with a statue depicting rounded, naked cherubs, spouting water into the fountain below. The moon above lit the open space and reflected off the pool of water.

Serene. Quiet. Peaceful.

Roderick could not enjoy any of what the picturesque garden landscape had to offer.

Not when his entire body tensed in anticipation of locating Lady Lucianna.

The only sound was his footfalls as he stalked farther into the night and away from the ball at his back. A rose thorn caught his trousers at his knee, digging into his skin and sending pain shooting down his leg as he pulled free.

The music from the betrothal ball had receded, as had any light given off by the terrace torches. The full moon afforded him little help as he passed under a topiary arch into yet another courtyard with benches and several statues—this time featuring animals.

Scanning the open area, Roderick looked for any

movement, listened intently for any sound that would betray Lucianna's whereabouts.

Nothing.

No movement.

No sound.

How had she disappeared so quickly without a trace?

Roderick refused to allow a sense of disheartening hopelessness to fill him once more. He'd lived too long with that weight upon him.

He'd seen no marked path leading to the townhouse drive and around to the street in front of the row of Mayfair homes, but there must be. Perhaps Lucianna had found it and fled the ball entirely.

It was time he returned, gave his good tidings to the betrothed pair, and departed.

There was time to find her on the morrow. He'd send his man to keep watch on her, and Roderick would approach her then.

He turned back toward the well-lit house set high above the gardens below, wishing it were possible to slip out of the party without notice; however, the growing crowd on the terrace told him his entrance had gained much attention.

Sighing, he started back, taking the same paths he'd taken when entering the gardens.

A wisp of midnight blue caught his eye as he passed by the cherub fountain.

Roderick didn't think, didn't pause. He took off after the figure as it fled back in the direction of the house. Catching her was not an option. He pushed faster, but she was more familiar with the paths as she turned and crisscrossed across the garden, her skirts gathered high to avoid tripping.

Triumph flooded him at the same time his irritation flared at having to chase the woman.

Roderick was knocked in the side of the head when he failed to duck under a low-hanging branch. He only allowed it to slow him for a mere second before pushing on.

Lady Lucianna was a few paces ahead of him now, her strides as long as his.

Not much farther, and the glow from the townhouse would light his way once more and he could increase his pace without threat of injury.

Exiting the garden path, Lady Lucianna veered sharply to the left and onto a walkway he hadn't noticed when he stepped from the terrace.

He lunged forward and grabbed her arm, halting her.

A quick tug brought her round to face him, and Roderick took her in his arms to keep her from breaking away.

Damn it, but she fit perfectly in his embrace. Lucianna's height nearly matched his, though she kept her eyes trained on his chest. Her silky, black hair was piled high atop her head, but Roderick longed to see it flow down her back.

He loosened his hold enough to bring his hand to her chin, nudging it upward, coaxing her to meet his glare.

She tried to pull her face from his hand.

"Look at me," Roderick sighed. The fight drained from him when a shiver went down her spine. Was she afraid—of him? "Lucianna?"

Reluctantly, she lifted her narrowed, moss-green eyes to him. They fairly glowed in the darkness.

"Why did you run?" he asked.

"I am not one to linger in the path of an angry man." She scowled up at him before turning to gaze at the terrace with disinterest.

She'd seen him, knew he was angry and looking for her, and so she'd run as opposed to facing the consequences of her actions. If she'd been a man, Roderick would have suggested they meet at dawn on the expansive lawns of Hyde Park to settle the matter between them. He would not have had to resort to chasing a female down during the middle of a social gathering.

His temper rose once more at her deception from that morning.

And her part in his ruinous fall from grace.

Not that his position as a duke was in jeopardy; however, there was a certain stigma that clung to a man who had been accused of unbecoming behavior with a woman not his wife or betrothed. It was easy, less complicated, to look the other way when a gentleman visited his mistress in private, but it was another thing entirely for the couple to be seen in public together.

Roderick had made the mistake of meeting his informant in a very public place.

He had caused the gossip; however, no one had thought to ask whom the woman was he consorted with, or what his relationship with her entailed. They would have learned that she was the wife of his father's dear friend—not a common harlot, nor his mistress.

The ill-advised meeting, and the gossip it had caused, would have lessened with time; talk of it replaced as another scandal occurred. But Lady Lucianna had decided to post it in the *London Daily Gazette* under the ludicrous guise of the *Mayfair Confidential.*

In one fell swoop, she'd stolen his chance to find out who was responsible for stealing his family fortune…and caused the end of his betrothal.

Roderick would not allow Lucianna to continue unscathed.

Glancing over his shoulder, he noted their proximity to the terrace. Happy to see that a few more people had joined the crowd watching them. From this distance, he and Lady Lucianna likely appeared in a loving embrace—a couple in the midst of a tender moment. However, they did not feel Lucianna's tense posture in his arms. They could not see the frown she turned on him. There was no way they saw the sparks of anger shooting from her glare.

"May I go, *Your Grace?*" she seethed, attempting to take a step back.

The woman was beautiful—an exotic, midnight rose.

But her hoyden ways and senseless destruction of his life were not acceptable.

Roderick pulled her close, causing her glare to snap back to his, her mouth opening in an *O* of surprise.

Yes, a lesson could prove very beneficial for Lady Lucianna in tamping her wayward tendencies.

And Roderick may be the best gentleman to do it.

He leaned down and took her mouth, his lips settling against hers.

Gauging her reaction, she did not pull away nor did her compressed lips soften under his. Roderick waited. If she jerked away, he would not stop her—he was not a brute. To his delight, she melted into him after only a brief moment, and he parted his lips, their mouths joining in a rhythmic dance of push and pull, give and take, exploration and conquest.

Everything around him faded away.

His entire body heated with the sensual movement of their caress.

When he ran his tongue across her bottom lip, her mouth blessedly parted, allowing him to explore further. He would show her how it felt to be trifled with, to have one's weakness discovered and exposed.

Tentatively at first, Roderick slid his tongue between her lips to taste her.

Honeysuckle and fruit berry. She was pure sweetness.

Everything about the night surrounding them faded to a distant memory.

He pulled her closer as his tongue set a rhythm with hers, much as their lips had, their bodies pressed tightly from knees to chest.

Lucianna fit perfectly against him—not too short, not too willowy.

His arm loosened, falling to cup her bottom as his other left her chin to rest on her neck, her skin soft as the finest cotton to his touch. In the moment, Roderick didn't long to have her—as had been the case at Bentley's—he needed her close to survive. Better yet, he craved to have every soft inch of her pressed against every hard line of his body.

His body was not only warm, it was on fire.

Lucianna pushed closer to him, demanding more, and Roderick gave it.

His entire body throbbed with need. Need for her.

The intensity grew to the height of severe pain.

Suddenly, his eyes sprang open as his tongue throbbed.

The blasted woman had bitten him—drew his tongue deep into her mouth and clamped her jaw shut.

His arms were suddenly empty, and the night breeze cast cool air upon his heated face. He stood alone, watching Lucianna flee down a path that ran parallel to the back of the house.

She paused several yards away. The woman would return. She would beg his forgiveness, and the entire wretched situation would resolve itself. Though he sensed his pride had taken the biggest hit.

Instead of making her way back to him, she settled her hands on her hips, her anger evident even from this far away despite the dim night and the barest illumination the moon cast on her.

"Your rakehell ways and heavy-handed manners will not prove my downfall, you scoundrel!" Her shout echoed across the space between them and rose up into the night as if the stars above sought to memorize her accusation and rain it down upon any woman who gained a familiarity with the Duke of Montrose.

She flipped back around, her black hair having come loose from its pins and cascading down her back as she lifted her skirts and ran.

Finally, she disappeared.

A loud cheer of celebration sounded from the terrace as the guests laughed at the scene he and Lucianna had unwittingly created.

He felt his mouth as she disappeared around the corner—thankful the hellion hadn't drawn blood.

Bloody hell. He hadn't meant to cause a scandal, only teach Lucianna the damage that could be caused by meddling in others' lives.

Taking in the sight of the terrace once more, Roderick set off at a leisurely pace down the same path she'd fled. He had no intention of catching her, only departing the party without attracting more attention. The entire walk, he pondered her accusation. A high-handed scoundrel and rakehell?

Roderick was nothing of the sort.

However, every person present with decent eyesight knew it had been the Duke of Montrose who'd stalked from the garden. He only hoped it was not too much to wish for that Lady Lucianna's identity remained a mystery, for if the *ton* recognized the woman he'd held in his embrace and kissed, there would be no chance of preventing the scandal to follow.

CHAPTER 6

LUCI CRINGED WHEN the door to the breakfast salon slammed open, then set her fork aside and took a sip of tea to clear her throat. The morning was early; however, that did not stop her father from moving through the house similar to an angry elephant. His rage had yet to diminish after the post in the *Gazette*, but neither had he taken his mistress out in public again.

It was a boon in Luci's mind.

She allowed herself a secretive smirk, keeping her attention focused on her plate. There was no need to incite her father's wrath while her siblings, Derek, Matthew, and Candace, were present.

The chair next to her at the head of the table was pulled back, and her father sat. Another footman set a heaping plate of pickled eggs, bread, ham, and cheese before him.

She glanced away quickly, at least confident it would not be she who brought the Marquis of Camden to anger first thing in the morning.

"Pickled eggs?" He pushed the plate away, causing his bread to slide onto the table and an egg to roll off his plate and across the pristine white linen between Derek and Matthew before finally hitting the floor.

Her mother, the marchioness, would be beside

herself when she saw the blemish on her rug when the thing broke open and spilled its yellow center.

The boys laughed, and Candace, Luci's youngest sibling, giggled.

Luci shot a warning glance in their direction. If they were not careful, the marquis' fury could just as easily land upon them. That was something Luci avoided whenever possible. They were too young to understand their father's shifts in mood and his black temper—or the destruction and injury that followed when someone continued to poke him.

A new plate was delivered to the marquis, and after a quick inspection, he proceeded to eat.

Her brothers and sister released a collective sigh. Even Luci gathered her fork and resumed her meal.

"May we be excused, Father?" Derek inquired. "I have studying to do. My tutor will arrive shortly."

Neither Luci nor her siblings knew the temperament of their father when he entered a room. If they did not request to be excused from their meal, the marquis would rant and rave about respect and proper etiquette. If they did ask to leave, their father was just as likely to punish them all for interrupting *his* meal.

From the set of her father's shoulders and his grim demeanor, today, the marquis was waiting and wanting an argument...no matter where he found it.

"Do you all think to scurry away the instant I enter a room?" the marquis seethed. "Oh, I am certain the useless lot of you will run off to your mother's side, pet her like an injured bird, and whisper sweet words of compassion to her."

"Derek, Matthew, Candace," Luci said in an even tone, making certain to keep her breathing regular, despite the anger seeping from her father's every pore. "Do hurry along and prepare for your tutors."

Luci kept her stare on her father, his head lowered over his plate, but there was no disguising the stiff set of his shoulders or his flared nostrils.

The door closed quickly behind the trio, leaving her to handle the marquis.

"Do you think to overstep me? Take command of this household?" His glare snapped to hers, their green eyes a matching set as the marquis attempted to stare her into submission and tempt her to break eye contact. "I am the lord of this house—and of your life. It would be wise for you—and your siblings—to remember that."

"I will certainly keep that in mind, Father." Luci notched her chin higher, refusing to look away or cower before him.

The marquis scrutinized her, his brow pulling tightly as he frowned. Luci was normally very cautious about saying the right thing to appease the man. And today was no different. She'd said the correct words, but her demeanor was not to his liking. There was a chance he would fall into a deeper rage. Or he could turn back to his meal, the fight over. One never knew.

However, Luci would not look away until he did one or the other.

She would never cower before him—never allow him to rule her as he did his wife.

Whether it was her own pride or her lack of self-preservation that kept her narrowed stare trained on her sire, she was uncertain.

Lucianna refused to be the broken woman her mother was.

She would not allow her father, of all people, to extinguish her flame.

It startled her how similar the man was to Abercorn. Though her father had never physically harmed his wife or children, he'd come close. Who was more dangerous? A man who did not hide his temper, or a man who remained calm and reserved at all times.

"Lady Lucianna?" The Camden butler, McMahon, cleared his throat. Neither nor her father had noticed the servant enter the room. "You have guests in the blue salon."

Finally, the marquis returned to his meal, and Luci made to stand, smoothing her gown as the footman pulled out her chair.

"Make yourself available this afternoon," the marquis muttered, slathering his toast with marmalade. "You will attend me at an important meeting."

"Yes, Father." Luci nodded. The marquis had never included her in a meeting, whether concerning his many business endeavors or those family-related. It was not unknown to the Camden clan that the marquis—and his decisions—ruled everything. "Do send for me when you are ready to depart."

She hurried from the room before her father could halt her for not requesting permission to be excused.

Edith and Ophelia were waiting in the blue salon.

Luci had expected them since she'd departed Edith's ball the previous night without notifying her friends. They had every right to be angry with her, but Edith appeared downright furious, and Ophelia…her face was red and puffy, her eyes filled with unshed tears.

"A-choo!" Ophelia brought a kerchief to her nose as she sneezed.

Edith set her arm around Ophelia's shoulder before turning to Luci. "Where did you disappear to last night?"

Luci recoiled at the blonde's angry tone.

It was usually Luci who raised her voice amongst the trio, and Edith who was collected, never daring to allow her decorum to waver.

"Yes." Ophelia sniffled. "I went to the cherub fountain, but you were not there. I waited in the cold for over an hour, calling for you, until I gave up and returned to the ball. And now—a-choo—I have a cold."

"Ophel—"

"Do not Ophelia me!" She wiped at her dripping nose before turning her glare back to Luci. "I am now sick—sick!—and for what? Where did you run off to?"

"You left my betrothal ball, Lucianna," Edith jumped in, her fury dimming to something closer to hurt. "It was an evening, only one night, to celebrate Triston and me—and you deserted us. For what?"

Luci proceeded into the room and sank into the nearest chair, the upcoming meeting with her father forgotten. It was Ophelia's turn to comfort Edith as she wiped a tear from her cheek. This was not at all what Luci had thought would occur when next she saw her dear friends.

"Please accept my sincerest apologies. I had no intention of leaving you out in the cold…or departing your ball." Luci clasped her hands in her lap, hoping she properly conveyed how sorry she truly was. Her head hung in remorse, but she peeked up at her friends, desperate to hear them voice that they'd forgive her. "I was in trouble. I had to leave or risk scandal for all of us. Please…"

Both women melted at the sorrow in Luci's tone.

"What happened?" Edith asked. "Ophelia told me it was Montrose who stormed across the ballroom. I didn't so much as set eyes on him."

"Oh, I tried to distract him." Ophelia coughed, swiped at her watering eyes, and continued. "But he marched right around me. Were you able to escape him?"

Luci was uncertain how much to share with her friends. Obviously, not how muscular and secure his arms felt as they held her. Nor would she speak of her desire to run her fingers through his silky black hair as he pressed his body firmly to hers, his hand cupping her posterior. And especially not that a pool of warmth had gathered between her thighs when Montrose had set his lips to hers.

However, she did owe them some form of explanation.

A smidgen of truth, without all the glorious details.

"Montrose kissed me!" Luci covered her mouth in

utter shock.

"He, what?" Ophelia yelped.

"The nerve of that scoundrel!" Edith's outrage would have been comical were it not for the sparkle Luci saw in her eye. Could her dear friend know precisely how much Luci had enjoyed their embrace?

"What did you do?" Ophelia's eyes widened, her hands pressed to her bosom, still clutching her kerchief. "This is much like a real-life novel!"

Luci sniffed. "Then it would be a gruesome one."

"Why?" Edith eyed her intently.

"Because I bit the fool."

"Bit him?" Ophelia sat forward, her cold forgotten. "Where? On his hand?"

"No." Lucianna shook her head, her hair loosening from its pins at the action. "His tongue."

"How in the heavens could you bite his tongue?"

Luci frowned—and Edith giggled uncontrollably— as the auburn-haired woman pondered how one could bite another's tongue. It was easy to identify exactly when Ophelia realized the only possible way for Luci to do such a thing.

"He…put *his* tongue…in *your* mouth?" she stammered, sending Edith into another fit of laughter. "But that would mean…"

"Yes, Ophelia." Edith patted the woman on her back when she sputtered, breaking into a sneeze. "The Duke of Montrose slipped his tongue into Luci's mouth. And, I suspect, she enjoyed the experience greatly— though she is obviously loath to admit it."

"I most certainly did not—"

Edith waved her hand, silencing Luci's protest. "Now, how did this kiss end in your deserting me and leaving Ophelia out in the cold?"

"Does he know we wrote the article about him?" Ophelia asked. "Oh, Lord Torrington promised not to tell, but Montrose owes us nothing, especially after we caused Lady Daphne to break off their betrothal."

"No, he did not allude to knowing about our activities as the authoresses of the *Mayfair Confidential*."

"Then why was he so angry?" Ophelia sat back once more, wiping at her eyes. "He was so furious, he almost ran me over in the ballroom."

"There was no time to ask before he kissed me, nor after I bit him." Luci hated her body for betraying her. Her face flared red, and that blasted tingling sensation between her thighs returned. She clenched her knees tightly together to keep the feeling from spreading. "That is when I ran down the path along the back of your townhouse, then down the drive to the alley, and home."

"*You* walked home?" Edith's brow scrunched.

"Of course. Do you think me incapable of finding my way home?" Luci retorted, offended by her friend's disbelieving tone. "We only live five townhouses from one another. Both of our stables back up to the alley. It was simple enough to reach my home and slip inside without notice."

It was Ophelia's turn to snort—as well as a woman could with her nose blocked by congestion. "You demanded your carriage follow you about the shopping district to avoid walking to the end of Bond Street to hand off your packages."

It was exactly what Luci had demanded on several occasions. "Last night was not a shopping excursion, I will have you know, though it will be necessary to obtain a new set of black ballroom slippers. Mine were utterly ruined by the mud and filth littering the alleyway, not to mention the dew from the lawns."

"What of your mother?" Edith demanded. "You must have worried her so."

"I sent word as soon as I arrived home that I'd left ill." Her mother was likely relieved to escape the ball early after her embarrassment several nights prior.

"And you did not think to have someone tell me—a-choo—I could come out of the cold?"

"Again, I am immensely sorry, O," Luci stood and then knelt before her friend on the lounge opposite her chair, taking her hands in hers. "I never meant for you to become ill, nor did I think I would need to go to such extreme measures to get away from the brutish man. What happened when he returned to the ballroom?"

Edith and Ophelia shared a questioning look.

"What?"

"I think we should tell her…" Ophelia glanced at Edith. "She should know."

Edith sighed. "If we must." Edith turned back to Luci. "A large gathering of guests witnessed Montrose kissing a woman in the gardens. They said she fled before anyone could discover her identity, and he left shortly after."

Ophelia smiled for the first time. "But now we know it was you."

"Is that supposed to make me feel better?" Luci demanded, releasing Ophelia's hands and returning to her seat. Her mind whirled with the possibility that someone at the ball had recognized her as she'd fled.

"At least no one suspects it was you." Edith's cheerful tone irked Luci.

"But Montrose!" Luci's mind was reeling. "He will pay for embarrassing me."

"Again, no one knows it was you."

"*I* know it was me. The rakehell has some nerve." Luci's hands balled into fists. "Yes, he will be seeking my forgiveness when I get done with him."

"I think it best you stay far away from the man," Edith pleaded. "What if he speaks the truth? You could be ruined—and put the *Mayfair Confidential* in jeopardy."

"All before we are able to prove Abercorn killed Tilda!"

"I can promise you, the man knows naught about our agreement with the *Gazette*." If Luci's friends noticed her words didn't hold any conviction, they didn't comment on it. "Now, I must ready myself. My father has requested my attendance at a meeting this afternoon. I must change my gown before he calls for me."

Luci stood, her friends following suit.

"Just promise us you will not say or do anything hasty until we know for certain exactly what Montrose knows," Edith said pointedly.

Shrugging, Luci embraced Edith and then Ophelia. "I promise to not act in a rash manner."

The women said their good-byes, agreeing to meet at Oliver's Book Shoppe the following day.

Neither Edith nor Ophelia noted Luci's phrasing: she would not act in a rash manner. But who determined if a manner was rash or well thought through?

CHAPTER 7

RODERICK SAT, NOT moving, behind his neatly organized, mahogany desk; at times, forgetting to breathe. He'd remained awake all night, pondering his situation and a way out of it—or, as best he could, a way *through* it. His drumming fingers broke the silence that had descended upon the room sometime that morning after he'd penned the letter to the Marquis of Camden.

Not a person had disrupted him in hours.

Though that did not stop him from jumping to attention at any little noise that penetrated his study door.

He'd informed his butler no one was to cross the threshold of his study until his guest arrived.

The solution to his many problems had been easily achieved, especially after he'd reassessed what actually needed fixing.

First, his financial status. He was low on funds; therefore, could not afford to keep an investigator on retainer. This made it no simple task to track down the men who'd played his father for a fool and left the Montrose estate with barely more than enough coin to keep the servants' salaries paid and wax for lighting. Yes, the key to rectifying this was far easier to attain than Roderick would have thought before the previous night.

His second problem would unwittingly solve his first. The hellion, Lady Lucianna. She was a woman in need of taming—and Roderick would be the man to offer for her hand. Their match—and her dowry—would not completely solve his financial woes, but it would give him ample funds for an investigator.

His chest tightened at the thought of possessing Lady Lucianna and all her fiery spirit.

No longer would it matter about the article she'd posted in the *Gazette* bringing scandal upon him. She had stolen his family's good name and honor with her foolish article, but now, she would correct the problems she'd created in his life.

If Lady Lucianna's father were as peeved by his wayward daughter as Roderick was, the man would willingly agree to the match. The betrothal agreement would be drafted with all due haste. The banns read as quickly as was allowed. Before long, both Lucianna and her dowry—a sizeable amount no doubt, if the Marquis of Camden's legendary eye for business deals and cutthroat ventures were to be believed—would belong to him.

The marquis would be gaining a duke for a son-in-law and have Lucianna taken off his hands.

And Roderick would insist that she reform her hellion ways or retire to the country.

Simple.

Now, he need only wait for Camden to arrive.

He glanced at the clock—nearly two in the afternoon. It wouldn't be long now.

Either the man showed, or he didn't, and Roderick was back to square one with solving his financial woes. However, if Camden came, all Roderick's dilemmas could be eradicated by mealtime.

He tilted his chin up and brought his arms up, interlocking his fingers behind his neck to support the weight of his head. All the while, his muscles relaxed, and he breathed easier, certain Camden would come.

He smiled. He hadn't been filled with an ounce of hope since he left the widow Cavendish the night before the scandal had hit. She'd agreed to meet with him several nights later and hand over the ledger of names, accounts, and bank locations for each gentleman involved in the damning ring of hells. Those lords had convinced his feeble-minded, gambling-and-drink-addicted father to hand over all of his family's fortune to invest in a new gaming hell in the Rookeries.

Roderick's grin faded at the memory. His father, the late sixth Duke of Montrose, had thought to settle his own gaming debts and invest in a business venture that would benefit his son—and his son's sons—for years to come.

He'd been utterly and unceremoniously swindled.

By men he'd likely considered his friends.

Men Roderick had never met nor knew anything of.

It was the main reason Roderick kept to himself. That, and he had no idea who was involved in the charade that now had him offering to wed a woman who he had little in common with, had only seen on two occasions, and who angered him to no end.

Lady Lucianna had thought herself cunning, no doubt. Luring him into the darkened gardens only to assault him and flee.

Little did the woman know Roderick was becoming quite adept at finding people and locating the information he sought. He was not his father, and would not be trifled with, especially by a mere slip of a lady.

Plus, he most likely would have already caught the men responsible for stealing his family's money if it hadn't been for Lucianna sticking her nose in his affairs. Or if finding the men were impossible, then he would have wed and used Lady Daphne's dowry to continue his quest for justice.

He massaged the ache in his neck. Maybe he should have sought his bed—or at least a warm bath and a change of clothes—after sending the missive to the Marquis of Camden. Roderick glanced to his liquor-stocked sideboard, longing for a tumbler to fortify his resolve; however, he needed to keep his wits about him if he were to best the marquis during the betrothal negotiations. His confidence was overly high his *guest* would not turn down the proposal.

A knock echoed from the foyer, and his grin returned.

Footsteps hurriedly moved to open the front door, and his butler welcomed Roderick's guest before the pair started in the direction of Roderick's study.

His butler's usual shuffle could be heard, followed by the solid, confident steps of Camden—and another, much lighter step. Had Camden brought his wife?

It hadn't occurred to Roderick that Camden would include anyone else. The match made sense on paper: the daughter of a marquis to wed a duke. Roderick's grin faded once more, and his jovial mood soured at the notion of convincing Lady Camden of his affection for Lady Lucianna.

LUCIANNA GLANCED AROUND at the gaudy, almost abhorrent foyer as the butler ushered them in. A large monstrosity of a chandelier hung overhead, dripping with dozens of candles. The floor shone as if it were waxed only an hour before. The table at her side was free of dust, and its vase filled with fresh, blue blossoms.

"His Grace is expecting you, my lord." The butler closed the door behind them, and a footman hurried forward to accept their coats. "Right this way."

Following her father, Luci moved deeper into the house. She had no idea whose townhouse it was nor why they were there. Hanover Square was an area even more prestigious than Mayfair, the houses far grander with sprawling lawns and extravagant gardens and stable houses. This property seemed a bit less cared for than others on the street, but nonetheless, its station was much loftier than her family home.

"Father?" She set her hand on his sleeve. "Who lives here?"

"You will find out soon enough, child," he snipped back, halting to take in her emerald gown, neatly pinned hair, and white gloves. "You should be thankful I have brought you along on such a momentous occasion." His brow furrowed. "As your father, I have every right to handle your future in any way I see fit."

Her future? She was only attending her first Season after the tragedy of her friend's death had cut her previous London Season short. As yet, no gentleman had shown any overt interest in her. Not that she planned to wed anytime soon. An honorable man was nearly impossible to find in a sea of scoundrels, rakehells, and rascals. Men drank too much, gambled exceedingly, favored women of the night, or lived day by day, hoping to keep out of debtor's prison.

Luci had no intention of being forever tied to an unsavory man.

With no suitors to speak of, she could only assume her father meant to sell her to the highest bidder—wealth, and stature—as a business deal.

Not uncommon and certainly not something she'd think was above her father's ilk. The Marquis of Camden was known for his vicious business dealings and cutthroat practices during venture negotiations. Luci owed him a bit of gratitude as he'd settled large dowries on both her and Candace. Though all that did was bring forth fortune hunters and men who would not give a whit about her once he held her money.

Every speck of common sense within screamed for her to beg her father to reconsider whatever matter had brought them to this house, plead with him to depart and never return.

Luci was helpless, a feeling she'd felt on one other occasion, a time she wished she'd tried harder to convince her friends and the magistrate that there was a villain in their midsts, not a grieving bridegroom. Very similar to the day Tilda had been pushed to her death, Luci was walking into a situation out of her control.

"Do not tarry, Lucianna." Her father glanced over his shoulder at her. "When a meeting time is set, it is highly improper to be late, especially with the significance of today."

The man's foul demeanor from that morning had vanished, replaced by a man who knew his worth and position. Confidence and arrogance dripped from his every word. The set of his shoulders was one of haughtiness. His easy manner told Lucianna that whatever awaited them in this home, her father was certain he held the upper hand.

And that terrified Luci.

No matter how much she despised her father, as the head of the Camden household, he was her master; just as he commanded and demanded respect from his servants, so were Luci and her siblings to follow his every edict.

She only need look to her mother to see the consequences if she ever actively sought to refuse her father's orders.

A shiver went through her at the penalties she'd face if the marquis ever learned it was by his own daughter's hand he had been exposed in the *London Daily Gazette*.

Luci squared her shoulders and notched her chin high—every ounce the daughter of the Marquis of Camden—as she marched down the hall after her father.

The servant opened a door at the end of the hall and announced their arrival. "Your Grace. The Marquis of Camden and Lady Lucianna to see you."

"Show them in, Danvers."

That voice...

Luci froze mid-step, every nerve in her body revolting against moving another inch. If she took another step, she'd enter the room, and her greatest fear would be realized.

"Come, Lucianna," her father hissed, stepping into the room and leaving her alone in the hall.

She suspected all color had drained from her face as icy tendrils reached toward every limb of her body.

The Duke of Montrose. They were meeting with the one man who more than likely knew all her secrets.

Luci suspected after witnessing Montrose's anger the night before that he'd stumbled upon her truth. The identity of the person behind the *Mayfair Confidential*. She hadn't been able to admit it to Edith or Ophelia that morning, but the fury Montrose had focused on her as he stormed through the garden could only mean he'd discovered she posted the article exposing his disloyalty to Lady Daphne.

The only thing left to do was stall him from telling her father.

Luci stepped into the room, greeted by Montrose's cocky grin of victory.

CHAPTER 8

RODERICK STOOD TO greet the marquis, his welcoming smile returning to cover his shock at Lady Lucianna's presence. Camden strode into the study, taking in the room around him before acknowledging his host. Lucianna was blocked from view behind her father.

Danvers gave Roderick a curt bow, and he nodded for the butler to depart and close the door.

This discussion demanded privacy, even from his household.

He knew full well what he'd asked Camden here to discuss, but Lucianna was a wild card. Roderick was uncertain if her father had shared the purpose of this meeting. If he hadn't seen fit to enlighten his daughter, it was possible she would be very upset when she learned of the reason behind the appointment.

Roderick did not want his entire household eavesdropping and spreading the news within the servant's gossip mill before an agreement was signed.

Hell, it might become necessary for Roderick to inform Camden of Lucianna's unsavory activities as the *Mayfair Confidential* authoress, which he was loath to do, as it could cause a scene within his house that would not be easy to mask.

Lucianna stepped from behind her father; her emerald gown matching her eyes, and her black hair framing her face angelically. Though Roderick knew from the glint in her eye that the woman was anything but angelic. Beguiling and witty, yes. Sharp-tongued and elegant, for certain. Demure, reserved, and modest, however, were not words he'd ever use to describe Lucianna.

She seemed as shocked to see him as he was to see her, and judging from the look of contempt that settled on her face, she was prepared to do battle with him once more. It was a shame they were not at Bentley's. He couldn't help but wonder who would have the upper hand this day.

"My lord," Roderick greeted Camden, refusing to allow his eyes to stray toward the marquis' daughter again. "Thank you for accepting my invitation to discuss this"—how to describe the matter at hand?—"delicate matter."

He risked a glance at Lucianna to see her frown deepen. It was the only sign the woman gave at her discomfort of the situation. He admired her ability to keep her emotions under such tight control, though the corner of her lips turned up in a confidence smirk.

Roderick was unable to harness his own shock, his brow lifting in a silent question as to what she found so comical.

"I see there is no need to introduce the pair of you," the marquis muttered. He looked back and forth between Roderick and his daughter. "Please, wait outside, Lucianna. I will speak with Montrose and call for you when we have settled on the details."

Her mouth gaped open as her face reddened. The woman was not used to being so easily dismissed, and Roderick would be fooling himself if he didn't admit he enjoyed her stunned expression.

For once in their brief acquaintance, she had no sharp retort, no sugar-dipped reply, and no way of refusing her father's command without causing a scene.

Lucianna, no matter her hellion ways, was still a woman born and bred into the highest society in England. She knew her role as the daughter of a marquis and played it well.

Would continue to play it well until she was no longer in a position for playacting. It was that time that should concern Roderick.

If she were anything like him, her memory was long, and her need for vengeance patient.

Finally, she nodded. "Yes, Father."

With arms crossed and one last lingering, scathing glare for Roderick, she turned on her heels and marched toward the closed door. She paused for the span of a single breath, as if expecting someone to jump forward and open it for her. When it did not happen, she reached forward and pulled the door wide, stepped out of the room, and slammed the door in her wake.

She was not happy. From Camden's slight cringe, he knew it as well as Roderick.

The marquis masked his irritation with his daughter by taking the seat before Roderick's desk. "Now, Montrose—"

"Do call me Roderick," he said. "If you are here, I assume my proposal is agreeable to you. We might one day be family."

Camden chuckled. Outright laughed in Roderick's face.

Roderick's brow rose. "Should I assume you are not here to speak about a betrothal between me and Lady Lucianna?" The hair lifted on the back of his neck, and his confidence lessened for the first time since sending the letter to Camden that morning.

The marquis sobered, eyeing Roderick. "Do you think you are the only duke sniffing around my daughter?"

Roderick sat heavily in his chair, taken aback. He hadn't even considered another offer for Lucianna's hand. "Well—I—I am certain it does not surprise me, my lord. Your daughter is charming and very beautiful, with quite possibly dozens of suitors clamoring for her attention."

"But she has the attitude of a dour matron, I assure you." Camden crossed his legs and reclined in his seat. "However, she is well-connected, schooled in the fine art of managing a household, and comes with a sizeable dowry. So, I should have expected the men to come calling, despite her less than agreeable nature."

Did the man not note the regal, graceful, perfection that was Lady Lucianna? Roderick supposed wealth did not lend itself to a keen eye for value and quality.

And make no mistake, no matter how angry he was at Lady Lucianna, how betrayed he felt by a woman who did not know him from the King of France, she was a woman of worth. It only took one look—and a few seconds in her presence—to know she was something special. Something worth having…and keeping.

"I must warn you, this auction may very well see a betting war the likes of Tattersall's best." The man chuckled again. "But before we speak of such important matters. Let us toast our new association with a drink."

Roderick leapt to his feet and moved to the sideboard, not because the marquis had commanded it, but for the sole purpose of hiding his flabbergasted expression—and growing anger—from the man.

The Marquis of Camden had just sat in his study and compared his daughter's betrothal negotiation to that of a horse at auction.

Devil take it, she was worth more than any horse!

Turning two tumblers right side up, Roderick filled each with a healthy portion of amber spirits. If the marquis' entrance was any indication, Roderick's afternoon would not be proceeding as expected.

Camden took his tumbler gratefully and sniffed at the liquor, as if the quality and age of the stuff would lend a good air on the man who'd served it. The brandy they held was aged longer than Camden himself.

How could Roderick have thought making a game of taking Lucianna as wife would be a simple, uncomplicated matter between two men?

Lady Lucianna was complicated at her core; a woman who fenced as well as any accomplished man, a lady who did not shy away from exposing her own father's misdeeds, and a hoyden who dared invite a gentleman to deepen a kiss only to bite down on his tongue.

"Now, I must admit, your offer to take the girl off my hands is much appreciated," Camden began, swirling the brandy in his glass. "I fear she has become a handful since her coming out—gallivanting about London, speaking out of turn, and Lord knows what else she does when I—or my staff—are not keeping watch over her."

Roderick only nodded in agreement. The woman was certainly entangled in far more than her father knew.

"And most recently, Lucianna has seen fit to turn my entire household against me. My younger children, always so obedient and well-mannered, have begun to challenge my authority and even look to Lucianna before adhering to my command. Honestly, I cannot have such mutiny in my home."

"My lord, I—"

Camden brought his narrowed stare to Roderick's, cutting off anything he'd thought to say in Lady Lucianna's defense.

"So, Montrose, in other words, I am very interested in your marriage offer. Unfortunately, I have gained another offer for Lucianna's hand, though I am not entirely hard-pressed to pick the better lord. She is like any wild filly. She will need a firm hand; possibly need to see the end of a whip every once in a while to keep her in line."

Roderick's skin crawled as if a thousand ants

marched along every inch of his body.

He was repulsed.

What father instructed his daughter's suitor to use cruel methods for harnessing her wayward tendencies?

The mere thought was baffling.

And Camden was obviously entertaining offers from other gentlemen. At least Roderick knew he would never raise a hand—or a weapon—against any woman, no matter how irritating their actions or words.

Roderick sat a bit straighter in his chair. Had another perspective husband agreed with Camden: a firm hand and a whip here or there when necessary?

Bloody hell, the marquis sickened Roderick; however, if he withdrew his interest in Lady Lucianna, she might very well be left with a man far less honorable than he.

Roderick would not forsake any woman to that fate—even Lucianna who'd stolen his only opportunity to find his family fortune.

However, marrying Lady Lucianna also meant tying himself to Camden.

He shuddered to think whom Lucianna would find herself betrothed to if it weren't Roderick. There were many cruel men living within London. Men who by no stretch of the imagination could ever be considered gentlemen. Men who spent their nights in scandalous brothels disguised as legitimate gaming hells. If a gaming hell could ever be *legitimate* in nature.

Lucianna was helpless to disobey her father's decision on whom she would marry.

"Ah, well." Camden emptied his tumbler in one swift gulp and slammed the glass on the desk between them. "I can see you are not the man for her. Which is a pity. I suspect Abercorn will have to do, even though he is as old as Corinthians."

The Duke of Abercorn?

What would the old duke want with such a young bride?

Neither alternative was acceptable. Turn away from a betrothal to Lady Lucianna and leave her in her father's clutches—and likely betrothed to Abercorn within a fortnight—or agree to Camden's conditions and be tied to Lady Lucianna and beholden to her father.

Roderick would never give the impression he'd abuse a woman, no matter what she may do to incite his anger; however, leaving her in Abercorn's clutches was the same, even if he were the one holding the whip.

"My pursuit of Lady Lucianna is very serious, my lord." Roderick commanded his shoulders to relax, to look at ease and not alert the marquis to the danger he was in even speaking of injuring a woman. "I am prepared to have the documents prepared and signed whenever you wish it."

"I will need to discuss it with my daughter. She is unaware of the nature of our business here."

Roderick wanted to laugh. He suspected Lady Lucianna was never fully unaware of anything.

"I have one request, my lord."

"Of course, Montrose." Camden stood, signaling their meeting was nearing an end. Roderick followed suit.

"I wish to call on Lady Lucianna." It had been many years since he'd attempted to court a woman. Even with Lady Daphne, it had all been arranged and handled behind closed doors. "I think it best she and I become acquainted more before we formally announce our betrothal."

"*If* you are to be betrothed," Camden corrected. "However, a stroll in the park or trip to Bond Street for ices would not be unacceptable."

"Very well. I will call on her presently." Hell, he would call on her this very evening, if it would not be seen as too eager. The last thing Roderick needed was for Camden to change his mind and give Lucianna to the Duke of Abercorn. "Shall we bring Lady Lucianna in and tell her about our agreement?"

Roderick wouldn't mind a bit of time in Lucianna's presence. Hell, maybe he would be so bold as to request a moment alone with her. They were to be wed, after all. Her father would be a fool not to accept Roderick's offer and nor could Camden be against allowing the soon-to-be betrothed couple a moment together.

"That will not be necessary, Your Grace." Camden shook his head and bowed. "I will inform her of my decision, and she will be prepared when you call on her. I will have my man draw up the paperwork for your signature."

"Of course, my lord."

There was nothing more Roderick could say or do as the marquis departed the room, soundly closing the door behind him. Truly, there was little Roderick suspected needed to be done at this time. Camden would handle informing Lady Lucianna, and when next they met, she would have no cause to deny him her company.

The sound of two sets of footsteps retracing their way back to the foyer was all Roderick heard as Camden led Lady Lucianna from the house.

For not the first time, Roderick wondered why the marquis had brought his daughter if only to instruct her to wait in the hall until they departed.

He refilled his drink and collapsed back into his chair.

He should feel a measure of relief to know that a formal betrothal between him and Lucianna was almost guaranteed, which meant his coffers would be full once more—or at least, back to a more agreeable amount—and he could resume his endeavors to locate the men responsible for stealing from the Montrose estate.

Relief flooded him. A bone deep sense of rightness filled him.

He would have his money—and Lady Lucianna.

His troubles were coming to an end. The

confidence that had filled him earlier returned.

CHAPTER 9

"WHAT WAS THIS all for, Father?" Luci asked as she settled her skirts. The carriage dipped as the marquis entered and took the front-facing seat. "Dragging me from the house only to wait in some lord's hallway seems peculiar."

Her father, ever the arrogant marquis, only stared at her before shouting to their driver to return them home. No matter her question or her rising temper, the man would not be prodded into answering any of her questions until he was ready to speak.

It was a trait Luci long suspected she'd inherited from the marquis.

She crossed her arms and stared out the window, prepared to wait for her father to speak. Arguing and insisting answers would get her nowhere. Maybe disinterest would lull him into a false sense of security, and he'd speak of what he planned to gain from meeting with Montrose?

Luci kept one eye on him. He didn't appear upset or furious, so Montrose hadn't spoken of the *Mayfair Confidential* and her part in the articles. She was thankful for that much.

Finally, her father sighed, and she turned from the carriage window to see him scrutinizing her. They were much alike, all darkness. Yet, Luci suspected her father's darkness was far deeper than surface level.

"You have been out of the schoolroom for nearly two years now."

Truly only fifteen months, but Luci kept that bit of information to herself.

"And you are spending my coin to furnish your second Season."

As if the Camden coffers were in jeopardy of running dry. Besides, Luci hadn't the time to spend any money beyond her basic wardrobe last Season before she and her friends went into mourning for Tilda. More accurately, Luci was enjoying just her third month as a debutante.

"Have you found a suitor to your liking?" he asked.

There it was. He wanted Luci to take a man to husband—and depart his household. The marquis would relish that. In one fell swoop, he'd have his hellion of an eldest daughter gone, and no one would stand in his way of treating his wife, Luci's mother, any way he saw fit.

It would be all the more satisfying when she delivered her next—and finale—blow to the marquis.

"I do not plan to wed, at least not this Season." After Tilda's death, and everything Luci had learned about the other unscrupulous men of the *ton*, she had little hope a decent man existed—with the exception of Lord Torrington. Plus, if she were to wed and move away, who would care for her siblings? There would be no one willing to step between them and their father's fury.

"Then we are both lucky I have found not one but two suitors for you." He picked a piece of lint from his sleeve as if his declaration were nothing more than him expressing his love of carnations, while Luci sat still—frozen—unable to process what he'd said. "Obviously, the Duke of Montrose is an influential, shrewd lord, who would make a great addition to the Camden lineage."

"You think to wed me to…Montrose?" Luci stumbled over the words.

"What did you think our meeting was concerning?" His tone said her father thought her dim-witted.

Luci hadn't given the meeting much thought beyond her father requesting her accompaniment, which was anything but normal. She and Montrose would make a most disastrous pair—she'd bitten the man, for heaven's sake.

"He requested an audience to discuss the joining of our two families." Camden spoke of her betrothal as if he were agreeing to discuss the purchase of a new carriage. "I cannot say I am against the match; however, I have other offers to consider."

That had Luci pushing back into the cushioned seat. "Other offers?" she squeaked, repulsed by the weak tone in her voice.

"Yes. Abercorn." He continued to gaze out the window. "Though I am uncertain if Abercorn is the man for you. Three wives and no children. What is to say you won't marry the man and grow old, never producing an heir—his Dukedom would pass on to another relative and forever be out of Camden control."

A business arrangement.

Her future had been reduced to nothing more than deciding what would gain her father more in the long run. A virile, robust lord like Montrose, who simply exuded potency and prowess. Or an aging, very wealthy duke like Abercorn, who would bring many business connections but no guarantee for a future including children who would be linked to the Camden name via their mother.

Luci shouldn't have thought any other option was open to her—unless she'd been able to stall long enough for her twenty-first birthday to arrive; however, she was two years from the date.

Montrose or Abercorn. Was that truly any choice at

all?

"Abercorn killed Tilda…and Montrose is a known rakehell," she hissed, gaining her father's full scrutiny. "You would make me choose between a murderer and a philanderer? You would enjoy that greatly, wouldn't you? Men of your own ilk, the pair of them."

"Lucianna!" he warned in a harsh tone. One that in her youth would have had her mouth clamping shut and her eyes averting to his feet. Not today. Not in this coach. And certainly not in matters dealing with her future. "You—and those silly, foolish women you call friends—caused quite the scene last Season. You are lucky either gentleman will have you. You are tarnished goods, to say the least."

She'd taken aim at her father and levied her most unforgiving insult; however, she'd said what needed to be said. If her father correlated her words with what had been printed in the *London Daily Gazette*, it would be a wonder.

Leaning back, Luci crossed her arms and turned her attention to the passing London street.

"Do not sulk, it will cause wrinkles," he mumbled. "You will marry either Montrose or Abercorn. Whomever I see fit to select for you."

Luci would rather a coin be tossed into the air to seal her fate.

"And if I will have neither?" she dared ask.

The marquis chuckled, a light, wheezy snort. "I did not raise a chit fool enough to think she has any say in whom I chose for her marriage. Do not be dim, Lucianna, it is very unbecoming."

"Abercorn killed Tilda," Luci said. Images of her lovely, bright friend lying lifeless at the bottom of Abercorn's staircase filled her mind. "You honestly cannot expect me to overlook that damning fact, no matter how *tarnished* you think I am."

"That was a sad, unfortunate occurrence. Do not think I completely lack sympathy for the girl. However, that is in the past. I am speaking for the future of the Camden name." His stealthy glare landed on her, almost begging her to argue further.

"Father, I…" She sucked in a deep breath to stop from sobbing.

"You will marry. And it will be either Abercorn or Montrose."

"And if I refuse?"

"Then I will drag you before the clergyman and see that the deed is done," he said with utter calm and composure. He was a man used to getting exactly what he wanted, when he wanted it. That he was prepared to hand his daughter over to a murderer, only meant gaining access to business deals that were before out of his reach. "Now, put a smile upon your face. We are almost home, and you will speak of your two suitors with vigor to your siblings. You will be overjoyed to learn whom I will ultimately offer your hand to."

"And then you will finally be rid of me."

Her father sat a bit straighter, an odd grin and faraway look entering his eyes. "Yes, yes, that is another boon I have yet to fully think through, though I will find great happiness in having you out from under my roof."

Luci could not blink, would not allow her father to think she would go quietly into a marriage she did not agree with—or any marriage at all.

But his stare matched hers in force. Her hurt mirrored in his determination.

Suddenly, the footman pulled the carriage door open.

They'd arrived at home.

"Smile, my dear daughter," he hissed. "I am certain you would not want to anger me into a hasty ceremony by special license."

Luci hated herself for giving in, but she smiled. This game was one of finely executed moves, parried by advanced defensive tactics.

Much like fencing.

And that was one sport she would always best her father at.

CHAPTER 10

ONE DAY.

One full day.

Roderick raised his hand to shield his eyes from the blazing sun. Well, it had been at least twenty-three hours.

That was an acceptable amount of time to wait before calling on one's intended, soon-to-be-betrothed.

Roderick slammed his hand into his jacket pocket to stop the shaking. His other held a large bouquet of yellow blossoms—he hadn't any notion the variety, but he felt like a coxcomb pacing before the Camden townhouse, scared to knock and face Lucianna.

The idea of her yelling and screaming at him was not what he feared.

No, he feared one question from her: why?

...and that would be the first time he'd be forced to lie to the woman he'd take as his wife.

Roderick would not tell her it was because he needed her dowry. There was no way he would be honest enough to tell her it was because he feared leaving her in Camden's household. And neither would he start off by asking her to write a retraction to the article in the *Gazette*.

Not that an apology from the *Mayfair Confidential*

would change anything.

Regardless, he was coming up to snuff. No matter what the marquis asked, Roderick was prepared to comply.

It struck him as odd he'd willingly agree to any conditions Camden set forth, but Roderick was appalled at his father's mismanagement of the Montrose estate— and he needed funds as soon as possible if he did not want his creditors to come knocking. What if his father had been working under the guise of doing what was right and honorable, but found himself waylaid in the process or even misguided by those he trusted?

The sleeve of his jacket moistened, and belatedly, Roderick realized the bottom of the bouquet had opened, and water was saturating his cuff.

Blast it all, but he shouldn't have gone through the trouble of procuring flowers…hell, what if she did not favor these exact blossoms? He would look like the fool he already felt he was.

He switched his hold to the other hand and shook his arm, water splattering the closed door in front of him, only leading to the continued leakage of moisture on his other sleeve.

Roderick leapt off the stoop to avoid more water marring the entrance. "For the love of—"

"May I help you, my lord?"

The tips of his ears heated, and Roderick shuffled his feet to hide the marks on the stoop. It was as if Cook had found him with his hand in the cookie jar.

He cleared his throat and smiled. "Good day. I am here to call on Lady Lucianna."

"My lady is not accepting visitors at this time."

As simple as that. Roderick had gone out of his way to do something special for the confounded woman, and she *was not accepting visitors.*

He fought to keep his temper under control. Circumstances had changed—he now needed her. Proving a point or teaching her a lesson was no longer important.

"I am certain if you give my name, Lady Lucianna will agree to see me." To help with his point, he held out the flowers before him and gave them a solid shake. "I would hate to see these beautiful blossoms waste away before Lady Lucianna has time to appreciate them."

The butler looked from Roderick to the flowers and back again, his brow pinched in a peeved manner before he sighed and held the door wide for the duke to enter.

"Whom may I tell her is calling?" he asked.

"Montrose!" Lady Lucianna's unmistakable hiss sounded from behind the servant. "How dare you—"

"I can call a footman to throw him out, my lady," the butler said, starting to close the door in Roderick's face, but he was already over the threshold, and the door only knocked his hand, the flowers falling to the stoop.

The servant's manners presented themselves once more. "Oh, my lord, allow to me collect—"

Roderick swatted the man away. "I can collect them without assistance." He knelt to the floor. "But thank you, all the same."

"What are you doing here, Montrose?"

Roderick cocked his head to the side to stare up. Lady Lucianna stood several feet behind the butler, her toe tapping as she pulled on her gloves.

"Your father gave me permission to call on you," Roderick replied, pushing awkwardly to his feet, the flowers once again clutched in his hand, although several blooms were either bent or missing altogether. "So, here I am."

"And here I go." Lucianna tied the strap of her hat under her chin and took her handbag from a side table. "I fear I have a previous engagement." She glanced over her shoulder and nodded. "Charlotte, come along before we are late."

"Lucianna!" The marquis' thundering voice preceded his solid footsteps as he descended the stairs. "Where are you—" Camden took in Roderick at the threshold. "McMahon! Step back and allow His Grace entrance. What is wrong with you? Take the damned flowers to the housekeeper."

Roderick nodded to the butler, regretful for his part in angering Lord Camden. "My lord. I was in the area and thought to call on Lady Lucianna, but it seems I should have sent word ahead, asking for an audience."

The man looked between Lucianna, buttoning her walking cloak, and back to Roderick, his arms damp from the flowers. "Where are you going, girl? I do not remember you asking for permission to leave."

Lucianna's chin lowered as if to convince everyone present of her meek nature. "I am to meet Lady Edith and Lady Ophelia at Oliver's Book Shoppe in less than an hour."

"You are taking your maid with you?" Camden's brow furrowed.

"Of course, Father."

"Then I see little reason why Montrose cannot go along, as well."

It was the first thing the marquis had ever said that Roderick agreed with.

Roderick smiled, clasping his hands behind his back and rocking on his heels.

"It is settled. Now, I have work to do," Camden nodded to Roderick and headed down the hallway with not so much as a "by your leave" for Lady Lucianna.

"Do not look so pleased, Your Grace." Lucianna pushed past him toward the door. "Come, Charlotte."

He glanced around the empty foyer—Camden had slammed a door down the hall, the butler had disappeared with the flowers, and Charlotte had followed her mistress outside.

Pulling the door closed, he followed the women to the drive. "We can take my carriage," he called, hurrying to catch up and assist the women, his driver caught off guard.

Lucianna halted, assessing his coach. "I think Charlotte and I would be far more comfortable in the Camden coach."

"Do not be stubborn, my lady," Roderick sighed, as the triumph of being included in her outing evaporated at her sour expression. "My coach and driver are ready and at your service."

She glanced at the conveyance, and Roderick expected her to turn down the offer; however, she surprised him by nodding and holding out her hand for assistance. Charlotte followed suit, and he entered the carriage last, galled to find the pair on the forward-facing seat. Roderick clamped his mouth shut, his teeth grinding, but he would not comment on the rudeness.

"Where to, Your Grace?" his driver called.

"Oliver's Book Shoppe off Bond Street."

At Lucianna's raised brow, he continued, "Do you think me so uncivilized that I am unfamiliar with local bookshops?"

"Humpf." Lucianna jerked her handbag onto her lap and busied herself flapping her fan.

Her maid had the good sense to stare out the window and act as if she were not present.

THEY DEPARTED THE carriage in much the same manner as they'd entered, with Lucianna hesitantly allowing him to assist her.

He then tucked her hand into the crook of his arm and pulled her close before whispering, "Do not bite again or you will fast learn I bite back."

Lucianna made to pull away, but he laughed and held her firmly in place. The woman needs must learn that while he was an understanding man, he would not put up with her hoyden tendencies.

Charlotte trailed them into the shop, a bell chiming overhead as they entered.

"Do wait for us here," Lucianna called over her shoulder as they walked farther into the bookstore.

The smell of worn leather and old ink surrounded Roderick, and he remembered his childhood spent in his grandfather's library. Shelves lined the room from floor to ceiling, each cluttered with books of every size. The hiss of conversation drifted on the air, and he noticed the shopkeeper and an older gentleman deep in discussion by the register. It had been a long time since he'd allowed himself the opportunity to wander rows of books, searching for adventure in written form.

"Are you looking for anything in particular, my lady," he asked as they meandered down a deserted aisle, putting distance between them and her maid. He noted the hair on the back of her neck prickle, exactly as he'd intended when he leaned in close with his last words. "I am here to assist you in any way."

"Do stop doing that," she hissed. "We are not in your private coach nor a secluded garden."

"But, nonetheless, alone." Roderick peered down the aisle and then back the way they'd come. "There is no one to see—or hear us."

Lucianna pulled from his grasp and turned her pointed stare on him. "That is very advantageous because I find I have much to say to you." Her glare traveled down his form and back to his face. "You are a scoundrel, a man in the habit of taking advantage of women when they are out of options. And I, Your Grace, will not abide by any of it."

"So, that is it?" he asked. "You will not *abide* by my offer, and instead, agree to wed old man Abercorn?"

"I have agreed to nothing, Your Grace."

"Roderick."

She stumbled a step at the change in conversion, her back pressed against a shelf of books labeled: *Adventure*.

"Call me Roderick. And I assure you, Camden is quite adamant you wed, and soon." He could not look away as her brow pulled sharply down, and then her face relaxed as if her thoughts were far away...all to return her eyes to him. "Come now, you cannot think a marriage to Abercorn would suit you."

"I am uncertain a marriage to any man will suit." She pressed her gloved finger to her lips as if she didn't trust herself to go on.

Blast it all, but he wanted her hands exploring his neck, tangling in his dark locks, and traveling down his back.

"However," she continued, drawing his attention back to the present—their reality, as it were. "I do see the merit in agreeing to your proposal." His spirits soared at her words, but why? "At least until I can find a way out of this nonsense."

Her meaning was clear: marriage to him was not to her liking.

"And marriage to Abercorn would be what, precisely?"

"Unthinkable." Her shoulders sagged. The weight of it all finally too much for her.

Roderick could imagine the taxing weight upon her given no option but to wed, and to select between two men not of her choosing. His betrothal to Lady Daphne had been done under similar circumstances; a duty to uphold his family's honor by securing the necessary funds to steer clear of debtor's prison. They'd made the best of their bad situation, he and Daphne. She was sweet, demure, and proper. Everything a man should long for in a wife; however, not once did he have the overwhelming sensation, the all-encompassing need, to take her in his arms and kiss her.

However, at this very moment, an irresistible craving drew him to Lucianna. He wanted to pull her against him, set his lips to hers, and give her the proper kiss he'd attempted in the gardens. However, this exotic

English flower came with thorns—barbs capable of mortal injuries to any man who attempted to pluck her.

The question was: Did Roderick think it worth the wounds to try and claim her?

"If I am unable to waylay my father or speak some sense to him, I will wed you, Montrose."

For the second time in as many minutes, Lucianna seemed to change before his very eyes. Her shoulders were now stiff with resolve.

"I am certainly happy you would choose me over the aging duke."

"I cannot say I did not consider many things in this decision."

"I would very much like to hear what sets me apart from Abercorn."

She eyed him closely before responding, as if gauging his off-guard manner before speaking. "Are you a murderer, Your Grace?"

"Not that I am aware of, my lady." He kept his voice neutral, refusing to show the shock that coursed through him at her absurd question. "Are you?"

She waved her hand and stepped away from the shelf. "Heavens no, do not be obtuse."

Him, obtuse? The woman had an odd way of deciphering who was being dim-witted.

She took his arm and continued down the long aisle, her free hand dragging along the spines of books as they passed. "Do you have a tendency to lie to your peers and the magistrate?"

"I cannot say the opportunity has ever presented itself, so I am unsure how to answer that question honestly."

"Are you for or against pushing someone down a flight of stairs?" Her steps slowed further with this question.

Roderick pulled her to a stop. Her eyes widened as if she sensed she'd gone too far—said too much. "What in the bloody hell are you speaking of?"

Lucianna averted her stare, remaining silent.

"For the love of all that is holy, Lucianna, what is this all about?" Roderick demanded. He reached out and placed his fingers gently on the side of her face, bring her stare back to his. "Lying…murder…what are you trying to say?"

She lowered her eyes, staring at his neckcloth. "These are all things Abercorn is guilty of."

"Then why would you write scandalous articles about others—false stories, mind you—thus ruining the lives of other men, if you know for a fact Abercorn killed someone?" Why this was the first question that came to mind, Roderick didn't know.

"You know of the *Mayfair Confidential*?" she breathed, her face going pale. "What do you know of anything?"

Her voice grew shrill—not an ounce of denial to be found.

An unspoken truth between them. Lucianna was behind the article that ruined his life…and now there was no denying he knew the depths of her misdeeds. She would not be offering any apology, just as he had no forgiveness for her.

"That is not important at the moment." Roderick pulled her close, the tip of her nose nearly touching his chin. "Did Abercorn murder someone?"

Her arm tensed under his hold, and she pulled her chin away, breaking eye contract.

It was all the confirmation Roderick needed. He did not need her to say the words. Lucianna was scared; of the situation her father had placed her in, and the likelihood she would be forced to wed the Duke of Abercorn.

Roderick would not allow it. Never had he harmed a woman. Never would he. Neither did it please him to see Lady Lucianna in such a terrified state.

CHAPTER 11

LUCI SHOOK HER head from side to side. She shouldn't have spoken of the events surrounding Tilda's death, or her hatred of the duke. She, with the help of Edith and Ophelia, was determined to see that Abercorn paid for his misdeeds.

Montrose would not interfere with that plan.

For now, allowing him to think she was in agreement with their betrothal would keep Montrose occupied, and her father satisfied—and Luci out of Abercorn's reach.

"Tell me what Abercorn did."

The duke's steel blue eyes drew her, wrapped her in a blanket of security. No matter how false that comfort was or how much she longed to tell him everything, Luci knew it was not true. She did not know him beyond his skill at fencing and his scandalous activities at the opera all those months ago.

Trust was something earned.

The Duke of Montrose had secured nothing with her.

"If you are in danger, I will handle this." He moved closer still, as if she were in peril in the middle of the bookshop.

His scent of sandalwood and oak washed over her,

and Luci breathed him in—deeply. She wanted to believe he would help her. Needed to trust she wasn't alone in her task to bring Abercorn down and make him pay for the loss of Tilda.

But, first, Luci would need to confide in Montrose...Roderick.

Luci was certain even her dearest friends were hesitant to believe her account of Tilda's fall down the stairs and Abercorn's hand in the matter.

Her father was well aware of her hatred for Abercorn but still thought to barter her hand in marriage to gain some measure of control. The marquis thought so little of his firstborn.

"If you wed me, you will be forever indebted to my father." She leaned back, needing distance. Surprisingly, she cared that her father would have some kind of hold over Roderick. "I cannot ever ask that of anyone. He is my sire, but he is every inch the horrid man Abercorn is."

"You cannot expect me to walk away after learning all this, not now." Roderick set his hands on her shoulders and gently caressed away the tension. "If he hurt another person, I am now bound by duty, and my honor as a gentleman, to see he is punished for his crimes."

A lock of hair fell loose from its pins, and Roderick brushed it back behind her ear, never taking his eyes from her as a shiver ran down her back.

Why did this man seek to help her?

Roderick owed her nothing. He was a pawn in her father's game to bring more wealth and prestige to the Camden name, just as she was.

"There is much you do not know about me—and my friends."

"I have witnessed enough to know you are not one to shrink away from the truth."

He was right, though she wished some days that she could forget Tilda, forget her wedding, and forget the gruesome sight of her falling down the stairs. Most of all, Luci wished she could forget the vacant stare from her friend's sightless eyes after her soul had left her body. Every moment, Luci dwelled on what she could have done had she noted Abercorn's ruthless, abusive ways before that night. Yet, as Edith and Ophelia repeatedly told her, none of them had noticed anything off with Abercorn—and Tilda had certainly not shared any disreputable things about her betrothed.

"None of this is your responsibility, Your Grace." Lucianna moved away from him. If she stayed near him another second, she would come to truly believe he could fix everything, repair her, and make certain Abercorn was brought down. There was no one who could see that happen but her—with Edith and Ophelia's help.

"If you will not tell me, I will search out my own answers," he called as she reached the end of the aisle. "I assure you, I will not stop until I find out exactly what happened."

Luci halted, clutching her handbag before her. Staring at the floor, she knew she had two options: step from the row and into view of anyone else in the shop or turn back toward Roderick. If she returned to him, she could not trust herself to keep her own secrets.

There was so much more to her than what Abercorn had done.

Roderick knew, or at least suspected, her involvement with the *Mayfair Confidential*. How could he tie himself to a woman who'd written such a scathing article about his scandalous behavior? Did he think to exploit her once they were unequivocally tied together?

And, more importantly, how could Luci even think to confide in a man guilty of such unsavory activities as being seen at the opera with a woman he was not betrothed to?

Her chin lowered.

She was no better than he.

They both had secrets; however, sharing hers would put her—and her friends—in jeopardy.

And Luci knew Roderick's secret. In fact, she'd made certain all of London knew it.

Why did a tendril of remorse flicker inside her? Never had she experienced even a hint of doubt or guilt over exposing gentlemen of the *ton* for what they truly were: scoundrels.

"Lucianna?" he pleaded. The raw nature of his tone pulled at her. Begged her to return to his side.

But for what purpose?

To enter into a sham of a betrothal to appease her father and keep Abercorn at bay.

Turning, Luci notched her chin high. "Lord Abercorn killed my friend. He pushed her down the stairs on their wedding night. I am the only person who saw the entire tragic scene clearly. And no one—with the exception of my friends—believes my tale of the events."

There. She'd said it.

Now she only need wait for him to laugh, chuckle at her absurd accusation. Roderick would insult her in similar fashion as her father; call her a feather-brained, dim-witted, reckless chit. There would be no need to start the charade of a betrothal because even a man marred by scandal would not allow his name to be linked to a delusional female.

Not that it mattered a whit to her. Luci didn't trust Montrose. It was far more likely she spoke of Tilda's death to push him away, not draw him close in confidence.

However, he didn't turn away from her. Nor did he so much as avert his stare or take a moment to think through what she'd shared.

Instead, he closed the distance between them, taking her into his arms and pressing them tightly together.

"Roderick," she breathed. "What in heaven's name

are you doing?"

"The only thing I know how to do...keep you safe."

His head dipped, and their lips met.

Not like before. Lucianna was not calculating her next move, preparing for a counter-attack, nor planning her escape.

She did not want to flee.

In fact, she wanted nothing more than to be lost in Roderick's embrace, sheltered from the cruel world around her. Away from the reach of Abercorn, and no longer her father's pawn.

Here, with the duke's arms wrapped tightly about her, and his lips upon hers, she could put the need for vengeance behind her. She'd never forget Abercorn's misdeeds, but they did not consume her.

Roderick consumed her now.

His embrace. His scent. His delicious, crushing hold on her.

It didn't matter that she'd ruined him before all of society.

It didn't matter she'd been tarnished by her need to publicly ostracize Abercorn.

Nothing mattered but his arms around her.

Luci was helpless to pull away, to push him away, to fight the connection she sensed forming with this man.

They needed to discuss everything: her involvement with the *Mayfair Confidential*, her spying on Lord Abercorn with her friends, and her father's need to control everything he touched. But not now, not here.

Luci's handbag fell forgotten to the floor, and she clutched at Roderick's back, pressing her entire length closer to him.

"A-hem?" The male voice cut through the haze surrounding Lucianna, and she reluctantly pulled back from Roderick, fearing the shopkeeper had found them in a most delicate position.

Glancing over her shoulder, it was not Oliver, the shop owner, but Lord Torrington grinning back at her, Edith at his side, while Ophelia hid behind the couple to mask her embarrassed and reddened face.

RODERICK FAIRLY GROWLED at the interruption when their lips parted.

As quickly and surprisingly as it had started, Lucianna leapt away from him as she stared over his shoulder.

His rebuff died on his lips when he turned to see a gentleman so large he filled the aisle with his sheer size, a petite blonde woman tucked into his side, and an auburn-haired nymph doing her best to hide from view behind the couple.

Roderick eyed the lady doing her best not to be seen. He had, in fact, seen her before.

"You." He pointed to her. "You were the one from the ball. You blocked my path and almost allowed Lucianna to escape."

"Which would make us," the massive man interrupted, "the couple whose betrothal ball you attended without invite."

"Lord Torrington, Lady Edith, and Lady Ophelia," Lucianna stepped in front of Roderick. "May I introduce the Duke of Montrose?"

"You may, but that will not be enough to pacify our curiosity at his presence." Lady Edith placed her hands upon her hips and scrutinized him as if he were a costly, rare bolt of fabric. One she hesitated to stare at for too long and didn't dare touch.

"Yes, Luci, what is going on?" Lady Ophelia asked, her head bobbing around Torrington's shoulder.

"I—well—he—" She glanced between her friends, a rosy hue blooming on her cheeks.

"I arrived at the Camden townhouse to call on Lady Lucianna. Unfortunately, my manners escaped me, and I did not send word ahead, asking for an audience." Roderick felt, rather than saw, Lucianna's eyes on him. "And so, I offered to transport her and her maid here."

Though if he'd known he was going to face a battle squad, Roderick may have departed the Camden townhouse alone, his flowers still in hand.

"Why were you calling on Luci?" Lady Edith pried, her eyes narrowing on him once more.

"It is a long story." He waved away her question. "But since you have arrived, I will bid you all ado and leave Lady Lucianna in your company."

Lucianna's arm shot out and snagged his sleeve, mercifully dried from the earlier flower incident. She held him in place at her side. "Montrose will remain. This is not as much his issue as ours. It seems my father is entertaining an offer from Abercorn."

"For what?" Lady Ophelia finally pushed in front of Torrington.

"For my hand in marriage."

Both women gasped, and Torrington's shoulders stiffened. "That cannot be true."

"I assure you it is, my lord," Roderick replied.

"The Duke of Montrose has graciously also made an offer for my hand." She glanced up at him for confirmation. When he nodded, Lucianna continued. "And, so, I will accept his offer…for now. But we must find the evidence we need to see Abercorn taken in by the magistrate. Then this whole charade can be put behind us and Roder—the duke—can return to his own endeavors."

"What in the bloody hell is that supposed to mean?" Roderick didn't have any other endeavors, at least not the emotional kind—or any other he was willing to share with Lucianna and her companions.

And why did he care if Lady Lucianna and her friends thought he was involved with another woman?

Three sets of rounded stares turned toward him.

The shopkeeper appeared behind Lord Torrington and the women, holding his finger to his pursed mouth, silently demanding silence.

"Oh, I find I like this man very much," Torrington barked with laughter.

"He does seem quite useful, doesn't he?" Lady Edith nodded in agreement.

"But he is rather imposing with his dark features and cold, blue stare," Lady Ophelia said, inspecting him from head to toe. "However, Luci looked like a storybook heroine in his arms. I could hardly tell where her black locks ended and his onyx hair began."

Were they seriously discussing *him* in front of *him*?

"Imposing?" Roderick could not keep up with the group's banter. "At least I am not the size of a bison."

All eyes turned to Torrington, not a single person mistaking *whom* he spoke of.

"Ah, well, I have been called much worse by a far lovelier person, Montrose. You need to do better if you think to wound my delicate sensibilities." He tapped his finger against his cheek in thought. "I believe an ox was the comparison, though that is very much in line with a bison. Oh, and arrogant and demanding, of course. Am I forgetting anything, my love?"

The blonde, Lady Edith, giggled, lifting on her tiptoes to place a kiss on Torrington's cheek. "I have apologized many times for calling you arrogant. I still stand behind my oxen reference, though."

"My lords, my ladies," the shopkeeper called, bustling down the row toward them, his own silence forgotten as his heeled boots clacked against the hardwood floor. "Please take your rambunctious assembly elsewhere, you are disturbing my patrons who are here for serious pursuits of knowledge."

"My apologies, Oliver, we will keep our voices down and not disturb anyone." Lucianna smiled at the shopkeeper, flashing her most angelic, innocent grin, and the man practically wilted where he stood. "If we promise, may we stay?"

Oliver eyed the group, his stare lingering on Lord Torrington a moment longer than the others before he conceded with a nod. "But keep it down, and don't clutter the row if someone comes looking for a book. I have bills to pay, after all."

"Of course, sir."

"We wouldn't dream of costing you business."

And finally, from Torrington, "Thank you."

"This way," Ophelia waved toward the back of the shop and pushed through the group, making certain not to make eye contact with Roderick. "There is an alcove toward the back where we can speak privately."

Roderick raised his brow at Lucianna, who only shrugged but followed her friends.

He hung back to allow the women to proceed him into the rear of the shop. That it allowed him a moment to take in the sway of Lucianna's hips as she linked arms with Lady Ophelia and Lady Edith was only good timing. With their heads tilted together, the trio of women whispered as they hurried to the alcove.

What wasn't as advantageous, was Torrington matching his slow strides, his hands clasped behind his back.

"They are a formidable group, are they not?" Torrington said in a low tone.

Roderick eyed the women, uncertain what he'd gotten himself involved in and what type of trouble awaited them. "Are they always this…aggressive?"

"Only when they have their minds set on something," Torrington replied, nudging Roderick onward. "Not long ago, it was me. Thankfully, now, it is…well, you."

"Me?" Roderick halted as they exited the row of books, and Torrington was able to step next to him as opposed to walking a step behind.

"Oh, make no mistake, Lady Lucianna has her

sights set on you."

The woman was confusing. One moment, she was running from him, the next she'd bitten him, and then she agreed to wed him. "Only a moment ago, she made it very clear she would only agree to a feigned betrothal."

Torrington patted him on the shoulder and turned toward the women, who'd each taken a seat on the alcove bench as they spoke quietly. "Yes, Lady Lucianna is a bit hard to read; however, she trusts you. It took her weeks to even speak to me."

Trust was an unfamiliar concept to him, so much more so since his father's passing.

"I thought this was all about Abercorn and finding proof of what he did…not that I can even say with any certainty what Lady Lucianna is accusing him of." He watched as the women's conversation became more intense as their voices rose. Lucianna scowled, and Lady Edith slashed her hand through the air, silencing everyone.

Torrington shook his head. "I fear it took me some time to figure it all out, as well, and it wasn't until the woman I love"—he tilted his head in Lady Edith's direction—"disappeared, that I wised up and took this whole Abercorn thing seriously. I'm uncertain if he is guilty of what they are accusing him of; however, the man is guilty of something dastardly."

"Do you think—"

"Triston." Lady Edith waved them over, her brow furrowed.

"We best join them before they decide to burn Abercorn's townhouse to the ground. Or something far worse."

"What could be worse than setting a house ablaze?" Roderick asked, his shoulders stiffening at the thought.

"Judging from the scowl on Lady Lucianna's face and the abject terror on Lady Ophelia's, I think we are about to find out." Torrington leapt into action far quicker than a man his size should be capable of and called over his shoulder, "We should hurry, before their minds are set."

Roderick caught up to Torrington as they both entered the alcove, the space having appeared far larger until they joined the women.

"We have decided how to proceed." The set of Lucianna's chin and her straight posture was all confidence.

"*They* have decided," Lady Ophelia interjected before her cheeks blossomed with heat, almost matching the hue of her long locks.

"There is no other option." Lady Edith set her hand on Ophelia's and squeezed. "Our time has run out, and we cannot risk the marquis favoring Abercorn's pursuit of Luci over yours, Your Grace. The Duke of Abercorn is known for moving quickly to secure what he seeks. His courtship of Tilda only lasted a fortnight before they were properly betrothed, the banns read, and a wedding date set."

"I still believe there is—"

"There is no other way, Ophelia," Lucianna cut off the woman's protest.

"Then what has been decided?" Torrington asked, lowering himself to the bench between Lady Edith and Lucianna.

Roderick ignored the spike of possessiveness that coursed through him at Torrington's proximity to Lucianna.

"We will knock on his door and simply ask him if he pushed Tilda." All three women nodded at Lucianna's proclamation.

"You think it is as simple as all that?" Roderick knew little about the old duke, but outright asking him if he killed a woman did not appear to be the most sensible course of action if they sought to discover what truly happened. "Why would he tell the truth now?"

"Because we plan to expose him in our next *Mayfair Confidential* column if he refuses to give us answers about the night Tilda died."

All four nodded in agreement as if writing a risqué column used to ruin men of the *ton* was not outlandish in any way, but completely commonplace among the group.

CHAPTER 12

LUCI STARED OUT the window as Montrose's coach turned into her drive and halted before her door.

The journey home had been tense, filled to brimming with awkward silences and averted eyes. Roderick, along with Lord Torrington, had venomously discouraged the women from confronting Lord Abercorn, especially in his own home.

A footman hurried to assist Charlotte down, but Luci waved him off when he offered her his hand.

She needed to speak with Roderick—privately.

Without her maid present, without the fear of an eavesdropping shop owner or her friends close to ask questions she didn't want to answer. In fact, it was Roderick who *owed* her answers.

And she would have them, even if she were forced to remain in his coach all night.

The thought sent a tingle through her as she touched her lips, no longer swollen from their kiss, yet she could still imagine the heat of his mouth against hers. Maybe all night with the intense man sitting across from her was not such a discouraging notion.

Luci shook the thought from her mind. Ever since he'd appeared at her door, flowers in hand, she sensed she'd judged him far too harshly and made assumptions inaccurately. It was a trait she despised in others, and she did not take kindly to it in herself.

"Your servant is waiting, my lady." Roderick shifted on the seat across from her. "There is little doubt the marquis awaits you across the threshold, as well, just out of sight."

"My father awaits no one, Your Grace." Luci reclined on the bench, setting her hands lightly in her lap. She was not going anywhere. "If he were home and had any need of me, he would simply drag me from this carriage."

She glanced toward the open door, and Roderick followed suit.

"See, the marquis is likely not in residence, or is ensconced in his study."

"I suppose you are correct," he conceded. "Your father is a formidable man. I think you take after him in that regard."

"That is highly insulting." Luci retorted. Never did she want to be her father—nor her mother, for that matter, but especially not her father. "The marquis is ruthless in business and merciless with his kin. He knows not the meaning of empathy or compassion. I would hope that is not the way you see me."

Despite all her agitated bluster, he only gave her a toothy grin and chuckled. The odd smile should have added a comical air to his appearance, but it only confirmed that there was a part of him Luci was unaware of.

But if she found out, what would that mean for her determination to see all unsavory men exposed and scandalized?

"While I know my status as an honorable lord has been called into question recently, I have not fallen so far as to think it acceptable or appropriate to insinuate that a woman is lacking in any way. I assure you of that, my lady." He sobered quickly at her narrowed glare and held up his hands, warding her off. "By formidable, I only meant undaunted by circumstance."

Her chest tightened at his words. That could only be taken as a compliment.

"May I ask you a question?" He sat forward, her answer seeming to hold immense weight. When she nodded, he continued. "Would it be improper to ask you to accompany me on a stroll down the lane? I find myself thinking you have many questions you wish to ask, and I cannot think to remain in this heated carriage overlong. I believe a spot of fresh air would do us both a lot of good."

Some time outside, still a private walk, but without the overwhelming urge to place her lips against his once more did sound wise.

She'd never been one to wilt into the arms of a man—especially one with a sordid past.

Admittedly, a disreputable past she had exposed…and was by the minute seeming unlikely for the man she'd come to know during their excursion to the bookshop. But how could she have misjudged him? He was at the opera with a woman who was not his betrothed. What explanation could there be for his action other than a scandalous one? Still, she had the feeling she'd been wrong about him.

"I think I would enjoy a stroll, Your Grace." *Roderick*, she thought to herself. Forever in her mind he would be Roderick. Not Your Grace, and certainly not the Duke of Montrose. "You are correct in assuming I have many things I'd like to discuss with you."

And many apologies to offer, though a mere spoken act of contrition could never repair the damage she'd done by posting the article in the *Gazette*. She'd still been grieving the loss of Tilda, wrecked with guilt over her passing. Bloody hell, she would forever be plagued by remorse at her dear friend's death; however, she could still attempt to make amends with Roderick.

Though he had every right to rebuff her.

He leapt from the carriage and held his hand out to

assist her down. "Shall we?"

"We shall." Luci couldn't stop from smiling at his gallant behavior.

She nodded to the footman when Roderick tucked her hand into the crook of his arm and led her back down the drive to the street beyond. There were no horses or carriages stirring up dust. No gardeners lingered in the yards of neighboring townhouses. It was as if they hadn't left the privacy of the Montrose carriage at all—until Luci noticed her maid, Charlotte, trailing at a discreet distance.

All thoughts of dragging Roderick behind the nearest shrub and imploring him to kiss her fled as they settled into a slow, steady walk. Besides her friends, Luci had never experienced such easy companionship. She watched over her younger siblings, but they were just that, brothers and sisters, not confidantes. She was their guiding light, and she struggled every day to search deep within to keep that light shining.

She had to be strong in every sense, or she feared turning into her mother; a woman so battered and beaten by years of neglect and harsh words she'd given up the fight. It was a pity Lady Camden, Eloise Constantine, once the daring, mysterious debutante had lost every ounce of fight within her.

That was not to be Luci's fate.

Her shoulders stiffened with resolve.

Never would she allow a man, any man, to bring her to such a low point. No matter if it were her father, a suitor, or the gentleman she pledged to serve for all her days.

But here, with Roderick, she could just be. Walk at her own pace. Remain silent if she so desired. There was no need for her to take control, lead the way, or carve a path.

She almost let slip from her mind the many nagging questions she had for him, in favor of simply enjoying this rare moment of ease. The late afternoon breeze pulled at her pinned hair, desperate to free it. The sun heated her skin, raining comforting kisses of warmth along her neck. A matching set of collared doves chirped and cooed from a tall tree as they strolled past. Roderick's hold on her arm tightened, tugging her closer to his side as if the breeze would blow her out of his reach, or the sun would scorch her delicate skin, or the birds would draw her attention too far from him.

In that brief moment, Luci was wanted. Cherished. Adored. She was worth more than her role as her father's bartering chip. Her sibling's protector. Her mother's champion. And Tilda's voice from beyond.

She was Roderick's prize. He was her protector. He would champion for her future. And he would supply voice when hers could not long speak loud enough to be heard.

Yet, he was still, in almost every way, a stranger.

It was nearly impossible to grasp that a man could stumble into her life and usurp her every thought. Make her long for things she hadn't wanted since her innocence had been shattered.

Since departing the coach, Luci had yet to dwell on their coming visit to Abercorn's townhouse. The overwhelming pressure to prove the man's guilt before all of society did not seem as all-consuming as a few hours before. No longer did she worry about Abercorn being the victor for her hand. Roderick, her defender, would never allow it.

He'd said as much, and she believed him with every ounce of her being.

She sighed.

"Do you wish to return home, my lady?" he asked, tentatively.

"Surprisingly, there is no other place I'd rather be than right here, right now." She stared ahead, scared to see his reaction to her forthright comment. Perhaps, it was he who wished to return her and be on his way. "Unless you have other matters to attend to?"

She risked a glance up at him from under lowered lashes. In the past, it would have been seen as coquettish, a feigned timid manner filled with doubt and reservations; but in this moment, Luci was terrified he did want to return her to her father's townhouse and escape the trouble she'd dragged him into.

"I have not another place to be today. Or any day, for that matter, Lucianna." He stared straight ahead, a pleasant smile overtaking his intense nature. "I think we have much to discuss, and the time is now before things progress further."

Luci was helpless to concentrate on anything after he'd said her name—Lucianna. The name had always signified the striking, rare, courageous woman she felt like on the inside. An outward sign to others that she was not a typical, pliable, demure maiden but something far more.

A woman destined to be remembered.

For her fierce love. For her loyal nature. For her invincible pride.

Not as a woman bought and sold at the discretion of any man.

Because of those exact qualities, she needs must make amends for the wrongs she suspected she'd done to Roderick. "What were you doing at the opera that night?"

His shoulders tensed, and Luci feared she had been right all along about him, that the disparaging accusations she'd levied against him in the *Gazette* were not misrepresented or false, but true.

"I was there seeking information." He kept his focus straight ahead as a coach turned onto the street and ambled by. "I was not there to be with another woman, nor did I ever seek to hurt Lady Daphne or tarnish her reputation."

"What type of information can be found at the opera?" She'd witnessed men, like her father, seeking out the willing, nimble bodies of ladybirds. She'd once stumbled upon a couple in an intimately scandalous embrace off a well-lit path at Covent Gardens. She was not fool enough to think that the sirens littering the playhouses and outdoor parks did not tempt gentlemen.

He sighed, and she sensed that he'd made an important decision, one he'd been debating since they started their walk.

Suddenly, the breeze blew no more, the birds were eerily silent, and a cloud passed over the sun, casting a large shadow over them.

"I was there to meet the widow of my father's best friend." He halted and turned toward her. "I was not there to betray Lady Daphne. Quite the opposite, actually."

"One might think it suspicious that a man would believe being seen in a very public setting with another woman on his arm would not harm the woman he is purported to love."

Roderick rubbed his jaw and pushed his hand through his hair. "I was thinking of none of that, only securing the information I needed to…" His words trailed off, and he dropped Luci's arm, pacing a few steps down the walk and pivoting to return and face her. "Lucianna, it was not my intention to bring Lady Daphne into the muddled mess of my life. Neither did I plan to levy that weight upon you. My family, everything my ancestors worked so hard for, was taken…and I have charged myself with getting it back."

Luci understood him a bit more in that moment. Roderick was searching for something, much like she was searching. "While that is very kind of you, it is my decision, as your betrothed, to decide what burdens I share with you and which ones I leave on your shoulders. I have little doubt we can assist one another."

He looked away, focusing on a house farther down the lane, and Luci feared it would be the end of their discussion. He would share no more and would refuse her help.

"I need to be honest with you. When I decided to offer for your hand, it was done out of a sense of vengeance, a need to hurt you—to take away your opportunity at a match of your choosing—much like your post in the *Mayfair Confidential* did to me."

He kept his eyes averted, but Luci was helpless to look away from the pain etched across his face.

She should feel an immense betrayal at his confession, laced with anger and outright indignation at his deceptive plans; however, none of these filled her.

"I know," she admitted. She'd known from the time she walked into his study with her father, though she'd tried to deny it, even to herself. "But what do you seek to gain from our marriage now?" Luci had little doubt Roderick would one day be her husband, the man who would protect her for the rest of her days.

And she longed to do the same for him.

His breath left him in a loud whoosh. "I wish I knew, Lucianna. Unfortunately, I've lived my life one day at a time since my father passed away, never planning past tomorrow because, well, the future is too bloody unpredictable. I thought I had things figured out that night at the opera, or at least, the means to sort through everything. But just as quickly, it was all stripped away."

"By my hand." Luci glanced down at the ground, ashamed of her part in ending his previous betrothal. "I am sorry you lost Lady Daphne."

He placed his hand beneath her chin and lifted her face, their eyes meeting. "While I cared for Lady Daphne—she is a sweet girl, everything that most lords require in a wife—we had nothing but a friendly fondness for one another. Love was not a part of our association, or at least, it hadn't matured to that point before our match was called off."

Roderick caressed her cheek, and Luci's eyes drifted closed, the warmth of the sun returning, his touch seemingly pushing the clouds away. It should seem scandalous to be so connected to this man, all while he spoke of his past fondness for another woman.

"In all our time together, I never felt for Lady Daphne what I've come to feel for you in the past several days," he confided. He placed a delicate kiss on her forehead before his hands fell away. "A coach is coming."

The words escaped him on a sigh.

Roderick had wanted to say more—and Luci was desperate to hear it.

Luci opened her eyes slowly, knowing once she did, whatever had been blossoming between them would need be stowed away for another time, another moment of privacy.

If and when it happened again, Luci would be ready.

Glancing down the street, she noted the Camden crest on the approaching carriage. From the quick manner in which Roderick put a respectable distance between them, he'd also recognized the coach and prepared for who would be within.

Luci turned toward the carriage and waved. There was no reason to hide—she and Roderick were doing nothing wrong. Charlotte followed them at a discreet distance, and it had been her father who'd suggested the duke accompany her for the afternoon. If anything, her father should be proud of her for coming to accept his dictates without further argument.

The conveyance slowed as it came abreast of them as they turned to return to the Camden townhouse.

"Good day, Father," Luci called with a smile when the marquis glared out the open window. "Beautiful day, is it not?"

Her father's scowl was all Luci needed to see to enforce that her jovial mood only irritated the man.

"Montrose," her father greeted Roderick curtly. "I thought you would have departed hours ago."

Why did he care if Roderick and she became better

acquainted? After all, if things continued down the path her father had set, they would be formally announcing their betrothal before long.

Luci had to applaud Roderick on his skill at playacting, as he grinned at her father, ignoring his dour stare. "We returned not long ago but, as Lady Lucianna commented, the day is too marvelous to spend trapped indoors. We decided on a stroll down the lane. You are welcome to join us for the return walk, my lord."

Luci nearly burst with laughter as her father recoiled in shock at the offer.

"Certainly not," the marquis said, leaning back into his coach. "Home, Rogers."

Without another glance, her father's driver put the horses back into motion, and soon disappeared into the Camden drive, several houses down the lane.

"Your father,"—Roderick pulled her close once more and set a slow pace—"he is a peculiar man."

"Is that another trait you will proclaim I inherited from him?" Luci let out the deep laugh she'd been holding inside. It didn't matter that her father thought he was using her as a pawn. She would not concern herself with worries over inciting her father's anger with her joyous mood.

No, for the next several minutes, Luci was determined to bask in the sun with the cool breeze on her face and Roderick by her side.

Tomorrow, she would fret once again about Abercorn and proving his guilt. When she sat down to her family supper table that evening, she would think over the truths Roderick had shared with her, and dwell on the secrets he still kept. As she prepared for bed that night, she would allow her own culpability in Tilda's death to wash over her and extinguish her spark of happiness. After Roderick's carriage had pulled away, Luci would reenter her family home to guide her siblings, protect her mother, and distract her father from his unavoidable fury.

But this moment, and the next fifty or so paces, belonged to her.

She lifted her chin to look at Roderick at her side and smiled—the most sincere grin she could remember since she'd watched her future shatter into a million tiny pieces as Tilda tumbled down those stairs.

"Your Grace," she sighed. "Thank you."

His brow furrowed in question, but he returned her smile. "What for?"

"For reminding me that it is acceptable to carve a moment out of life to stop—or stroll—and appreciate the warm sun, the call of the birds, and the afternoon breeze in my hair."

Silently, she added, *And the kiss of a most dashing man.*

CHAPTER 13

"STOP FIDGETING, OPHELIA," Luci scolded as they arrived at the Abercorn townhouse stoop. "We have yet to even knock on his door. He will see through our ruse if you keep that up."

The girl was a nervous Nellie if she'd ever seen one, afraid of her own shadow, and prone to picking at the stitching of her gowns. Despite all that, Ophelia was Luci's dearest friend since Tilda's passing, and she loathed putting her in this predicament; however, they all needed to confront Abercorn.

Edith patted Ophelia's shoulder. "Everything will be all right, do not worry."

"There is no need to coddle her," Luci hissed. "If the pair of you would have agreed to expose Abercorn in the *Gazette* months ago, none of us would be here right now."

"You cannot possibly know that," Edith snipped.

"Oh, I most certainly do know that."

A whistle sounded behind them, letting Luci know that Roderick and Lord Torrington were in place, keeping a close eye on the trio from the shadows of Torrington's father's townhouse, directly neighboring the duke's property.

It reassured her to know Roderick was close and

would allow nothing to happen to her. He didn't have to say it. After their time together the day before, Luci was confident Roderick had more in common with Lord Torrington than her father. He was not guilty of what she'd accused him of—escorting his mistress to the opera while betrothed to another. She would do what she could to polish his tarnished reputation. But right now, she had to keep her focus on Abercorn.

"Is this the best place to speak with him?" Ophelia tugged at her gown. "We saw what happened the last time we were in his home."

"There is no other place the man will be as complacent—feel as secure—as in his own surroundings." Edith and Luci had heavily debated this part of the plan, deciding that approaching the duke in a crowded ballroom or at the opera would not lead him to speak freely. "Besides, we have all agreed to remain downstairs."

Luci was confident in their decision to confront Abercorn, even though Ophelia appeared so nervous she'd likely fall over at the littlest breath of trouble.

"Are we ready?" Edith asked, plastering a smile on her face, ever the fearless one since she'd fallen in love with Torrington.

"As ready as we will ever be." Ophelia fanned her reddening cheeks.

"Remember"—Luci eyed both of her friends—"we are here to speak with Abercorn about his generous offer of marriage. This is a purely social visit with you both serving as my chaperones. Everything is above reproach."

"Until we get our feet in the door," Edith whispered.

"Exactly." Lucianna grinned.

Their plan was as solid as it could be. After they had entered Abercorn's townhouse and were led to a receiving salon, the women would make certain the drapes were pulled back, allowing Roderick and

Torrington a clear view to keep watch over the trio.

If anything went awry, they would kick in Abercorn's front door, if necessary, to reach the women.

Luci knocked on the door, and footsteps were instantly heard from within.

An elderly butler pulled the door wide, his eyes scrutinizing the trio.

"Lady Lucianna Constantine, accompanied by Lady Edith Pelton and Lady Ophelia Fletcher, here to see Lord Abercorn." Luci handed the butler her calling card, determined that they not be turned away. "Is the duke receiving visitors?"

At the butler's continued silence, Luci worried Abercorn was not in residence at all and their carefully crafted plan would be thwarted by their own mistake.

The servant finally stepped back, holding the door for them to enter.

Edith and Ophelia both sighed with relief.

Luci glanced over her shoulder as the two women entered the Abercorn townhouse. Roderick gave her a reassuring nod.

Their idea may very well be harebrained and without chance of success, but at least Roderick had enough faith in her to allow her the opportunity to lure the truth from Abercorn. There was no doubt Roderick had his own secrets. She'd be a fool not to notice the way his shoulders appeared to hold the weight of a thousand pounds or the hard lines around his eyes, a product of sorrow and loss. Or the way he analyzed everyone as if outlining every way they could injure him if he allowed them close.

Luci shuddered to think she'd caused some of that burden with her piece in the *Gazette*.

"My lady?" the butler asked when she remained on the stoop. "This way, please."

Putting Roderick from her mind, Luci entered the foyer, surprised by the many candles lighting the area. It was certainly a waste of coins to burn this amount of wax on a daily basis.

The servant shuffled, his feet never actually leaving the floor as he walked across the foyer and opened the room to a similarly lit salon. Upon entering, Luci was pleased to see the drapes were open, and a clear view of Lord Torrington's father's townhouse was in sight.

"I will let Lord Abercorn know of your presence. His Grace will be with you momentarily." He bowed stiffly as the women glanced about the room. "I will ring for tea. Do have a seat."

He pulled the door closed on well-oiled hinges, leaving Luci to inspect the room as Edith hurried to the window and waved in Torrington's and Roderick's direction.

The salon was decorated in bold shades of yellow and blue, complete with striped drapes, polka dot pillows, and matching plaid lounge and stuffed chairs. The obnoxious sight had Luci's head swirling at the odd pattern contrast and color combination. Upon closer inspection, the pieces in the room, including the tables, lamps, and wing-backed chairs close to the hearth appeared fairly dated. Even the pillow on the lounge was frayed at the edges.

This room had been appointed long ago, likely before Abercorn was out of the schoolroom.

Edith and Ophelia selected a low-slung sofa in sight of the large, arched window, remaining visible to the men outside, while Luci continued to stand. She was unsure why, but something told her standing was the best way to face the opposition.

And Abercorn was most certainly their opponent.

Luci would not allow herself to be fooled into a false sense of security based on her friends being near and Roderick being just outside the window. That was exactly what had happened to Tilda. The duke had presented himself as an honorable, kind, and worthy lord when he held none of those traits.

If she were utterly honest, the man might have duped any of them into marriage.

A shiver went down her spine to think it could have been her lying at the bottom of those stairs—or Ophelia, who would have been even less likely to defend herself than Tilda.

No, Abercorn would not remain free to harm another woman, especially Luci.

She would take Lord Torrington's suggestion and run off to Gretna Green before she'd allow her name to be forever linked to Abercorn. Though wasn't it already? She'd caused the scene at the duke's country manor, demanding the magistrate investigate Tilda's fall and pointing the finger at her friend's new husband.

Luci crossed her arms in defiance. She would sound the alarm again without a second thought—only this time, she would protest louder…and longer. Until Abercorn was removed from polite society and never given another opportunity to harm someone.

Tears stung her eyes.

Poor Tilda.

Again, they should have noted something not quite right about her bridegroom.

But Luci hadn't…and her friend had suffered the consequences.

"Lady Lucianna, my dear. What a charming surprise."

She pivoted in time to see Abercorn enter the room and close the door behind himself.

"And Ladies Edith and Ophelia?" He paused, his stare widening on the women sitting close to the window. "I must say, this is *very* unexpected—but in a good way, nonetheless."

"Your Grace," Luci said, dipping into a curtsey. "My father spoke of your betrothal offer, and I thought it time I pay you a social visit."

Both Edith and Ophelia sprang to their feet and dipped low in greeting. Luci couldn't help but notice the duke's eyes stray to Edith's bosom as she curtseyed.

"No matter the reason." He waved his hand, dismissing her words. "It is a pleasure to have you all in my home. I know there is much in our past; however, I am certain it can all be discussed with time—and a measure of patience. Please, do have a seat."

Edith and Ophelia looked to Luci with hesitation, but she nodded, and the pair regained their seats by the window. She noted Edith glance toward Torrington with a weak smile. Blessedly, Abercorn seemed preoccupied and didn't appear to notice Edith's fascination with the landscape beyond the windowpane.

Luci followed suit and sat upon the lounge, facing her friends and hoping the duke would take the seat across from her. That would put his back to the window and allow her friends' attention to go unnoticed.

She crossed her feet at the ankles and arranged her skirts, biding some time before it became necessary to speak. The cushion crackled with disuse beneath her when she shifted to tuck her feet under the lounge.

"Your home…" Luci paused, debating how to continue. She was loath to insult Abercorn before he'd even begun speaking. "It is very antiquated."

Outdated and in need of renovation was what she'd been thinking; however, antiquated was the best she could do.

"Yes, well," Abercorn sighed. "My mother renovated this townhouse, selecting every piece from the wall sconces to the rugs, even hand-stitching the pillows in this room, and I am hesitant to undo all her hard work." He glanced around the room, obviously attached to the yellow and royal blue trimmings with many years of fond memories. Finally, he returned to the present. "Of course, once I take a wife, she will have control over the entire household, and an unlimited purse to make any changes she deems necessary to make this her home."

Abercorn sat a bit straighter in his chair as if

expecting her to applaud his generosity and kind nature. His lips pulled back in a wide grin, showing off his stained teeth, yellowed almost to match the furniture his mother had selected decades before. Could she have guessed what the man would be reduced to in his old age?

"It would please me greatly if you'd accept my courtship, Lady Lucianna—or may I call you Lucianna? Mayhap Luci, as Tilda was fond of calling you?" The man appeared a hound waiting for a well-deserved treat.

A pain stabbed deep at her middle, as if the man had used his words to stake her. The duke did not deserve to utter Tilda's name—not today and not ever.

Abercorn would receive no reward from her. "Lady Lucianna will do fine."

"Very well, but you have leave to call me Francis." Reclining in his seat, the duke glanced at the door. "My apologies for my staff's inadequacies. I thought tea would have been delivered long before now. You all must be parched." He stood, pulling the servants' bell cord several times. "Another item my wife will be charged with rectifying."

"Tea is not necessary, Your Grace," Ophelia chimed in from her seat by the window.

"Of course, tea is necessary, far more than that, it is expected." He tugged at the cord several more times before returning to his seat, avoiding her wrinkled nose and pinched lips. "It will not be long now."

The charade was wearing thin on Luci, and the tension was growing thick—it seemed only Abercorn hadn't noticed the unease in the room.

"Lord Abercorn, may I speak freely?"

He broke eye contact as he smoothed his necktie with a chuckle. "Lady Lucianna, England has known several female monarchs. No matter what the colonists spout, our country is a progressive state. Women have the right to speak of what they wish, just as men, especially with a man who—with luck—will one day be your husband."

Edith burst into laughter, drawing Abercorn's attention as if he'd been so absorbed with Luci he'd failed to remember they were not alone.

At Luci's scowl, Edith clamped her mouth shut and stared at her lap, but her blonde curls bobbed with silent mirth.

"Thank you, Your Grace," Luci said with a grin, luring the duke's attention back to her. "It is only I wonder why you seek to wed *me*."

His expression grew pensive as if even he hadn't thought about why he desired to court his dead wife's best friend. Rubbing the back of his neck, he glanced at the door once more, but there would be no reprieve from her question.

The door remained solidly shut.

And her question hung openly between them.

"You see, while Tilda and I were very close, we are also exceedingly different people." Luci couldn't help but acknowledge the many dissimilarities between them. Tilda was sweet, caring, and compassionate—a true English rose of pure innocence. In contrast, Lucianna was, admittedly, jaded, cynical, and not the least bit demure. Not to mention, Luci's insistence that *he* had pushed his new wife to her death. But all Luci could verbalize was, "She was petite with hair of the softest brown and eyes that matched, while I…well, we can all see I am nothing like Tilda with my midnight locks and moss-green eyes."

It was almost insulting to both women to reduce their differences to the purely physical—meaningless, skin-deep, external attributes.

The duke cleared his throat, the direction of the conversation causing a gleam of perspiration to break out across his forehead. "It is, well, that is a rather difficult question to answer; however, I will endeavor to do my best." His hand twitched, and he reached out to smooth the fringe on the side of his seat.

"It is not a difficult question at all, Your Grace." She bit the inside of her cheek to hold back further comment.

"You are quite stunning in a dark, exotic way. Also, well-connected with the grace and poise I seek in my future wife and duchess," Abercorn declared with a satisfied grin, as if comparing her to a bird trapped in a gilded cage was a future any women would seek out. "You are witty, intelligent, and possess a strong will I admire greatly. We would make a fine match—the marriage-minded mothers will be envious of your ability to catch a duke, as it were."

Luci swallowed back a smart retort. The man certainly was daft if he thought she would pay any mind to his flowery words.

A fine match, indeed.

She forced an innocent smile, relishing the spark of unease that lit his face.

CHAPTER 14

RODERICK LEANED AGAINST the three-story townhouse at his back and crossed his arms, keeping his stare on Lucianna through the window. Lady Edith and Lady Ophelia sat close to the arched panes, hardly taking their focus off Roderick and Torrington.

The sun was high overhead, the eaves from Torrington's family home shielding them from the harsh heat of noonday. He took his eyes off Lucianna perched on the lounge in Abercorn's home for a brief moment to take in the bright blue sky above. Since their morning sparring match at Bentley's, not a single rain cloud had dared cross the London landscape—this fact had not escaped his notice.

"We never should have agreed to allow them anywhere near Abercorn without us present." Torrington sighed heavily, pacing in the shadows of his father's townhouse. "Anything could happen before we are able to get to them."

While nervous, Roderick was confident in Lucianna's ability to care for herself. The blasted woman had bested him with a foil and survived all these years under the control of Camden. She was no demure, fragile creature.

However, Torrington's lovesick, puppy dog

demeanor, fretting over Lady Edith's decision to accompany Lucianna and Lady Ophelia into the duke's townhouse was fast growing cumbersome and annoying.

"If it would make you feel better, you are welcome to press your nose to the windowpane, mayhap you will even hear a bit of the conversation," Roderick jested. "Oh, and you can look upon Lady Edith with your smitten stares of affection."

He half expected the man to round on him and throw a fist at his face, but instead, he chuckled, breaking the tension that had stiffened his shoulders. "Is it so apparent?"

"Is what so apparent?"

"That I can hardly take my eyes off her for a moment."

"Only to anyone blessed with sight." Roderick wanted to reach out and halt the man's pacing, but instead, he turned back toward the window.

"This is not a normal occurrence for me, I assure you," Torrington gushed, turning once more. His feet trampled the vegetation as he continued his stalking. "It took nearly losing the bloody woman for me to realize I'd fallen unequivocally in love with her."

"So you mentioned." Roderick casually pushed away from the wall, attempting to hide his interest in the direction of their conversation. "What happened?"

The question halted Torrington mid-stride. "Lady Lucianna did not tell you?"

He shook his head.

"You did not read of it in the *Gazette*?" Torrington's brow rose in question.

"If I had, I now know not to believe a word of it," Roderick said with a shrug. "Likely, Lady Lucianna did not see it as her place to share."

Roderick was loath to admit that, in fact, they'd had scarce moments alone to discuss anything more serious than the matters transpiring between them.

"My father's wife kidnapped Edith and absconded with her to her family's Southend home, determined to toss us both over the cliffs to our deaths."

He waited for Torrington to laugh at his joke, but his expression remained serious.

"Your mother did—"

"Not my mother," he corrected. "My father's third wife."

"Why in heaven's name would anyone wish to harm Lady Edith?" Roderick inquired, suddenly feeling the need to pace himself.

"She thought Edith and I had spied her with her lover," Torrington turned his attention back to the window—and Lady Edith's copper stare—and Roderick feared the man would fall silent, but he continued. "But, with Lady Lucianna's and Lady Ophelia's assistance, I rescued her…and then Lady Lucianna rescued all of us from scandal with her story about a carriage accident and my gallant appearance to save them from a night stranded along a deserted country road."

"What happened to your stepmother?"

"Oh, she has since retired to the country and will never cause Edith harm again."

"I would suspect her lover has noticed her disappearance," Roderick prodded.

When Torrington didn't immediately answer, Roderick turned toward him, fearful he'd insulted or angered the man, but Torrington only nodded to the window. "It doesn't appear as if Lord Abercorn is pining away for his lost lover."

"Abercorn?" Roderick didn't even attempt to suppress his shock. "Your stepmother's lover was Abercorn?"

"Afraid so," Torrington nodded in confirmation. "And to make matters even more scandalous, my stepmother, Esmee, was once *my* betrothed…until she took a liking to my father's title and decided not to wed me and wait to become a marchioness instead."

"And I thought society eyed me with concern," Roderick mused. "If I keep you by my side, I never have to fear they are staring at me."

Their chuckles were cut short by a loud crash and two female screams.

"Bloody hell!" Torrington shot into action, not pausing a single second to see if they could deduce what had caused the commotion. He was already running toward Abercorn's front door—with Roderick close behind.

Within a few yards, Roderick passed Torrington, his feet pounding down Abercorn's cobbled drive. It didn't matter who saw him thundering toward Abercorn's door.

They'd taken their focus off the women for only the blink of an eye.

And something had gone seriously wrong.

Roderick didn't bother to knock or await the butler's answer. He gasped the door latch and pushed. Thankfully, the door was unlocked, or Abercorn would have returned to the foyer to see a splintered, used piece of wood that could no longer be confused as a door.

The entrance was dripping with candles, and the sconces were lit along the three halls Roderick glanced down. It was a bit odd for only an afternoon social call. Even the chandelier above held the maximum candles, glowing brightly and gleaming off the polished floor.

"What are you waiting for?" Torrington shouted, knocking Roderick on the shoulder when he continued into the foyer and turned left toward the salon the women had been shown to. "They are this way."

Bloody hell, but Roderick knew which direction Lucianna was in. Even if he hadn't been watching from outside, he was drawn to her. Her very essence called to him. She was a siren—his very own siren.

Torrington flung one door open, but the room was empty.

Roderick hurried past the man and opened the next

door with a bit less force.

"Lucianna?" Roderick stepped into the room, taking in the sight surrounding him.

Lucianna still sat on the lounge, but Lady Edith stood near the window, her hands clutching at her throat. Lady Ophelia trembled, eyes wide as she fanned her face, the color having drained from it. But he didn't spy Lord Abercorn as his narrowed stare surveyed the room—though it was possible the offensive color scheme played tricks on his eyesight.

"What is going on?" Abercorn called gruffly, his head popping up from behind the lounge Lucianna sat upon. "Why, I never—"

"I can ask you the same thing, Lord Abercorn," Roderick thundered, the tone so deep and menacing it shook the portraits on the walls. "What is the meaning of this?"

Lady Edith stepped hesitantly around Abercorn as he struggled to push himself to his feet, and she hurried to Torrington's side. They began to whisper between one another, but Roderick couldn't take his attention off Abercorn. The man was dangerous, Roderick was certain of it.

He was at Lady Lucianna's side within the blink of an eye, and he took her hand, pulling her to her feet and dragging her into his arms. "Is everything as it should be? I was so worried."

"I am well, Roderick, I promise."

He could barely hear her words over the thrashing of his pulse, but he pulled her tighter to him, his embrace only softening when she pulled away to stare over his shoulder.

Lady Ophelia gasped and collapsed onto the bench near the window, and the color drained from Lucianna's face, leaving her looking green.

Thundering footsteps sounded from the hall, entering the room behind him.

"Lucianna, girl," the Marquis of Camden's voice

boomed into the room. "What is the meaning of all this?"

"Father, I—"

"Your daughter," Abercorn said, back on his feet and moving closer to where Roderick continued to hold Lucianna, though not as closely as he'd like. "Arrived a few moments ago, her two friends in tow"—Abercorn paused for a moment, nodding to both Lady Edith and Lady Ophelia—"to accept my proposal. She said she is honored to become the Duchess of Abercorn. I fear I was so overjoyed, I tripped over a settee in celebration."

"What?" Lady Ophelia exclaimed, jumping from her seat on the bench.

"That is preposterous," Lady Edith shouted, setting her hands on her hips.

"That is not at all what transpired," Luci said, pulling away from Roderick to stare at her father, her head shaking back and forth. "I would not accept Lord Abercorn's offer of marriage."

"Then what is happening here?" Another woman, far more matronly than Lucianna and her friends, cut in. The adornment on her hat bobbed precociously as she pushed her way into the room and rushed over to Lord Abercorn. "Are you hurt, Frannie?"

Roderick looked to Lucianna and then Torrington, but no one seemed to know what in the blazes was going on.

"Oh, do not fret over me, Sissy," Abercorn pushed the woman's hands away. "I am only filled with excitement and was not careful enough. Can you believe Lady Lucianna has agreed to be my wife?"

Abercorn and the elderly woman shared a quick embrace before *Sissy* placed a quick kiss on the duke's cheek and receded back toward the door—where Camden still stood, silently watching the room.

"There is a mistake. This is a mistake. Abercorn is addlebrained," Lucianna said, moving toward her father. "I was not here to accept Abercorn's proposal."

"She is only embarrassed to be caught in my home by so many." Abercorn chuckled. "She is such a delicate lady; however, there is no need to keep hidden what we have any longer, Luci."

Roderick wanted to pull Lucianna back to his side and punch Abercorn in the jaw at the same time. Unfortunately, only one was possible.

"I assure you, Lord Camden,"—Roderick grasped Lucianna's arm, but he didn't need to tug to have her return to his side—"Lady Lucianna and her friends were not here to accept any form of courtship or betrothal from Abercorn."

Camden's shoulders stiffened, and his narrowed stare landed solidly on Roderick as if he were the unsuitable, unwelcome occupant of the room.

"Lucianna," the marquis seethed, never taking his glare off Roderick. "What is the meaning of this? I did not instruct you to call on Lord Abercorn, nor did I allow you to spend more time with Montrose. Did you seek to thwart my plans, much like you do in our home?"

He advanced on his daughter, but Roderick took a step also, pushing Lucianna behind him as he held up his hand. "Lord Camden, allow us to sit down and discuss this—mayhap without so many prying eyes?"

"I do not see what we would need to discuss," Abercorn blustered, looking between Camden and Lucianna, the first hint of doubt crossing his face. "Lady Lucianna and I are ready to make our betrothal official. Camden and I were just in the library going over the agreement."

Roderick's stomach sank when Camden made no move to deny Abercorn's words.

"Father," Lucianna said, her voice laced with hurt. "Tell me you have not decided my fate."

CHAPTER 15

LUCI DID HER best to glare at her father, but inside, she was falling apart, crumbling, caving in. She blinked rapidly to hold back the tears that threatened to cascade down her face. Crying before Roderick was bad enough; however, she adamantly refused to allow her father or Abercorn to see her weaken. Or show any sign of giving up.

The situation had spiraled so quickly, Luci could barely understand what was transpiring. Her father had made it seem as if he were pushing Luci toward Montrose as a suitor when all along, he was set on Abercorn. But why? There could be very little besides an added two decades mingling with the upper crust of society that Abercorn had to offer her father.

And there was no doubt, the Marquis of Camden's goal when marrying off Lucianna was to increase his connections; both within society and in the business. It begged the question: what had Abercorn offered Roderick could not?

"Things are decided," her father said with a confident nod. "I think it best if you and your *friends* leave, and you return home. I will arrive shortly to speak with you."

She didn't like the way he sniffed at the word

"friends" as if Edith and Ophelia were little more than rodents riding her coattails.

"I will not leave, Father," Lucianna seethed. When she felt Roderick's hand caress her arm, she cooled down a bit. "I have no intention of wedding Abercorn."

"That is not up to you," Abercorn said with a smug smile before looking to Camden for confirmation, but his grin fled when he saw the scowl on the marquis' face. "What I mean to say is—"

"It does not matter what you mean, Abercorn," Camden hissed, for the first time allowing his cool demeanor to fall. "Who I choose for Lucianna is my decision. Neither of you has any say in who that is—nor when things will be officially settled."

It was the only bright spot in the conversation. Abercorn had sparked her father's displeasure, and Luci only hoped it was more than the transgression her father laid upon her shoulders. Maybe he would see reason, understand that in no world should she be required to wed a man who might very well have killed her dearest friend.

"I think it best if Montrose, Abercorn, and I speak privately." Her father pivoted sharply and stalked from the room, expecting Roderick and Abercorn to follow.

Abercorn and her father had given her matching smiles, and Luci swore they would have continued with an explanation of letting men handles the business at hand while the ladies returned to their tea and needlework.

Abercorn and Sissy were the first to snap into action and hurry after the marquis. "My lord, we can use my study, if that pleases you."

"Do keep your nose above trouser level, Francis," her father huffed.

Luci held tightly to Roderick's sleeve, knowing she should allow him to go—to speak with her father quickly and not cause the marquis' anger to settle on him if he were tardy to the study; however, she needed to speak with him.

There were many things they hadn't discussed, namely, their association after this feigned betrothal ended. Was he even willing to continue with the charade?

More importantly, could Luci ask him to make that sacrifice?

Once their betrothal was called off, Roderick would face another round of scandalous gossip—once again caused by Luci and her petty actions. There would be no chance that Roderick would forgive her twice for ruining his chances of securing a wife.

"Roderick, please…" She looked up into his eyes, eyes she'd always seen as icy and closed off, but now, they appeared crystal blue with a hint of desperation. "I cannot wed Abercorn, but neither will I expect you to throw away your future to save me."

A reassuring squeeze on her shoulder brought Luci's attention to Edith and Ophelia, both at her sides with looks of determination. Even Lord Torrington's dour scowl spoke volumes.

"I—we—will never allow Abercorn to get his hands on you," Roderick assured her, taking her icy hands into his warm palms. "We will think of something."

"If all else fails, the pair of you are welcome to my original plan to wed Lady Edith," Torrington offered with a grin, but it quickly faded when he realized the stark expressions on everyone else's faces. "Honestly, it is a solid plan and would not be hard to see done."

"I agree with Triston," Edith said with a nod. "Gretna Green may be the only answer."

"Gretna Green?" Roderick stared between Torrington, Edith, and Luci. "But that would mean—"

"We would actually have to wed," Luci finished, shaking her head. "I cannot ask that much of you, Roderick. A fake betrothal is one thing, but a legally binding marriage? I could never ask you to sacrifice so much."

Nor was Luci certain she could live with such a grand sacrifice on her part. A future with Montrose as her spouse, neither having agreed to the match willingly, could very well prove a disaster.

"But we will not know anything until Montrose meets with the marquis and Lord Abercorn." Ophelia's low, hesitant words cut through the many emotions flooding Luci. "Let him meet with your father. Then we shall convene again and decide our next move."

"Since when did you become the voice of reason, Ophelia?" Edith asked, clinging to Torrington's side.

Ophelia's brow rose. "Likely since you became so smitten with Lord Torrington your sensible nature has been all but forgotten. Besides, I have always been infused with much sense, though I rarely need express it. That is what I have you and Luci for."

Nervous laughter filled the room as the group started toward the door.

"I think you all should wait at Lord Torrington's father's townhouse," Roderick instructed as they entered the foyer. "I will meet with the marquis and join you immediately after."

"I will stay here with you." Luci pushed her shoulders back and paced toward the study door that stood ajar, not bothering to glance behind her to see her friends depart or Roderick trail her.

This was her life—her future—and she would not see her fate decided by her vengeful father or Abercorn and his delusional, self-absorbed tendencies. Neither man was the least bit concerned with her well-being or happiness.

"Slow down, Lucianna, or you will stumble and injure yourself." Roderick grabbed her arms to halt her, but did not hold her so tightly she could not pull away. She adored that about him—he wanted her to listen to him, yet he would not force his ideas, concerns, or opinions on her.

Roderick *did* care about her happiness.

Of that, she was certain.

He might even willingly sacrifice his future to make certain Abercorn never touched her.

What kind of woman would Luci be if she allowed him to throw away his life to make certain she wasn't forced into a marriage not of her choosing?

He stared down at her, imploring her to stop and listen, but Luci couldn't do that. If he spoke, gave her all the many reasons he should go through with their betrothal, Luci might be convinced to allow him to sacrifice himself. Hell, after their walk yesterday, she'd even led herself to believe he actually cared for her beyond the retribution he sought for Luci's hand in ruining him.

For those many minutes, Luci envisioned a future wrapped in his arms, always safe and protected. She dreamt of a home all their own—and children with their midnight hair. A girl with her father's intense blue eyes, and a baby boy with Luci's moss-green irises.

Both were tanned beyond what was proper because Roderick insisted they spend a great deal of time outdoors, picnicking in the park or hiking the trails along the Thames.

It was foolish and self-serving to even think about the possibilities and future to be had as the Duchess of Montrose.

"I will come with you to meet with my father and Abercorn." Every muscle in her body tightened, but Luci refused to allow her calm demeanor to slip. "I think my father will listen if I am present."

RODERICK STARED INTO Lucianna's deep green eyes—taking in the desperation and hurt that lingered just below the surface of her calm exterior. He had no right to demand she depart with her friends, nor ask her to wait outside the study.

The marquis and Abercorn were, even now, discussing Lucianna's future. Something her father may legally have control over, but not if he sought to hand her off to an unsavory, despicable lord. No woman should be lowered to play the pawn between gentlemen.

Roderick's honor as a nobleman would not allow such a thing.

Luci was everything any English gentleman should long for in someone they called wife, though not because of increased social status, or wealth, or even because of her exquisitely dark beauty. She had a wit superior to most men, the smarts to know her own worth, and the cunning to make her own way if her father's chosen path did not suit her.

"We will confront your father and Abercorn together," Roderick compromised. It was Lucianna's decision in the end. "But if you feel the need to depart at any time, we will leave together, as well."

When she nodded, a lock of hair came loose from her pins and hung down along her cheek to caress the top of her shoulder. For not the first time, Roderick longed to run his hands through her unbound hair and bring the long tresses to his nose. They must certainly smell of lavender or vanilla.

There would be time for that. Bloody hell, but Roderick would make certain there was plenty of time together in their future. Their brief walk hadn't been enough. His chaste kiss to her forehead was not nearly sufficient to extinguish his desire for her. Not even a fortnight wrapped in her embrace, staring into her deep, complex, green eyes, with unlimited hours talking about their pasts, the present, or the future they envisioned for themselves would satisfy him.

She grasped his arm, notched her chin high, and squared her shoulders, signaling that she was prepared to face her father.

Roderick wished he felt even a small measure of

the confidence she displayed as they walked the several paces across the foyer and entered Abercorn's study.

Even together, they were on uneven ground—the advantage going to Abercorn.

Roderick pledged silently to take that benefit from the other duke.

Entering the room, Lucianna pulled close to his side, Roderick realized he'd held the upper hand the entire time. Abercorn may have his title, his wealth, and his many business ventures, but Roderick had Lucianna.

On his arm, at that moment. And if he had his way, every day hereafter.

Roderick had successfully broken through the tough exterior Lucianna had built up to keep her heart safe from both her father and others who meant her harm.

The way she held his arm tightly, her fingers squeezing through his sleeve, told him she'd allowed Roderick in, expecting him to reinforce any weak spot in her defenses. And bloody hell, he was loath to disappoint her.

"Camden." Roderick nodded before turning to Abercorn, who scurried behind his desk, a place of perceived safety, no doubt. "Abercorn."

"Lucianna," Camden said, his narrowed glare settling on her. "You will depart immediately and await me at home."

Lucianna stiffened. "I will—"

"Lord Camden," Roderick cut in, giving Lucianna a reassuring smile. "Lady Lucianna has a right to be here. This is her future we are discussing. Do you not believe she should be heard?"

Camden lifted his palm loosely as if to say it mattered naught to him before he turned away and took one of the seats before Abercorn's desk, leaving only one chair open. "Sit, Montrose."

Roderick led Lucianna farther into the room and pulled the chair out for her to sit as he stood behind her.

It was as much to show Lucianna the respect due her—that these two men ignored—as it was to keep Camden off guard during the coming negotiation.

"I see no reason for Lady Lucianna and Montrose to be present." Abercorn tapped a stack of papers on the desk surface before him. "The agreement has been drawn up, reviewed, and only needs your signature, my lord."

"While I partly agree with you, Francis," Camden spoke slowly, "I do not agree the present agreement is acceptable."

"But that is not what you said before Lady Lucianna and her friends arrived."

"That was before I was aware of the seriousness of Montrose's pursuit of my daughter." Camden sat back in his seat, folding his hands in his lap as if greatly satisfied by the change in circumstances. "Two men, dukes no less, seeking Lucianna's hand in marriage? I think it best I retire and allow you both to meet with your men of business to submit new agreements if your goal is to call my daughter wife."

Roderick snorted.

The man actually expected a bidding war to ensue for Lady Lucianna's hand. Roderick did not disagree that she was worth the effort on both his and Abercorn's parts if they wanted to pursue her. However, she was being treated like cattle whose highly valued lineage and sires demanded men offer all they had to own her. These men, Abercorn and her father, seemed not to realize the priceless value of his midnight English rose—but he knew all too well.

No one would ever own Lucianna.

Not even Roderick.

CHAPTER 16

WHAT OF MY heart? Lucianna wanted to scream as Charlotte led her to her bedchambers. The maid kept up with a litany of mumbled nonsense, "There there," "Get some rest," "Allow the men to handle things," and the most infuriating, "Your father will choose wisely."

Luci didn't remember bidding Roderick farewell nor entering her father's coach.

A servant steered her clear of Lord Torrington's family townhouse and made certain she was settled before the conveyance took off toward Mayfair.

Now, she sat at her dressing table as Charlotte brushed out her hair as if Luci were preparing for bed. It was only late afternoon. A time when fashionable men and women were strolling in the park or shopping on Bond Street, not being carted away by the powers that be—namely, her father—without so much as a fight.

She was a beautiful, fragile bird in a cage made for two—her mother and her.

Luci snorted. She'd truly thought to escape it all, carve her own way in life, never being reduced to that of a captive. The many times she'd underestimated her father had finally caught up with her. The overwhelming pain in her chest told Luci her determination had waned to desperation. And, finally, hopelessness.

She looked around her childish room with its frilly, lilac bedding and matching pillows. The window drapes were several shades darker, more of a violet. The hues should clash, throwing the room into disarray, as a pure lilac color was no match for an overpowering dark violet. However, her mother had insisted that every piece of furniture in the room be white—pure, untouched, and innocent.

Had Lady Camden tried to reclaim her own innocence as she'd designed this room when Lucianna was in short skirts and pinafores?

If it had been Lucianna's choice—and nothing thus far in her life had been—she would have decorated the room in dark burgundy with blue accents, and the occasional gold trimming. The room would evoke a need to bow to the power held by its occupant.

However, the castle did not make the king.

It went much deeper than that. It was a sense of rightness everyone around the sovereign felt with such a man in power. The security of knowing that the correct person could be trusted to make a well-thought-out and conscious decision that would benefit all.

No matter how hard she attempted to take control of the situation with Abercorn, her friends questioned her. No matter how many times she'd declared she would not wed that murdering lord, Luci felt her voice blowing on the breeze, heard by no one.

Not *no one*, precisely. Roderick was aware of her wants and needs.

He was conscious of the fact that Luci would rather run to the wilds of Scotland than be joined in matrimony with Abercorn.

Did he suspect she had no such aversion to him as her husband?

Secrets and all, Lucianna still cared deeply for him. Even now after such a short time. It was his wounds, the ones he'd shared with her on their walk, and the many he still kept inside that drew her to him. However, long after the mystery of him vanished, she would want Roderick still.

A tap at the door had Charlotte setting down her brush and hurrying over to open the portal.

The housekeeper swept into the room with a full tea service, but the wooden slab did not close.

Luci tilted, narrowing her eyes on the darkened hallway beyond, as Charlotte prepared her normal cup of tea: Earl Grey, cream, and one lump of sugar with extra-hot water.

When not a sound came from the hallway except for the receding footsteps of their housekeeper, Luci focused on her beverage, which Charlotte held out to her before resuming her chore.

Lucianna closed her eyes as the brush moved through her long locks with nary a knot or tangle. It was much as she longed for her life to be: predictable, even in course, with only the occasional concern. She didn't want a life plagued with arguments, doubts, hardships, and, worst of all, regrets.

It was the main reason she pushed so hard to prove Abercorn's guilt. Until that day came, she would be weighed down by regrets, held down by daily reminders that she'd failed her friend not only in life but also in death.

"Lucianna?" a quiet voice called from behind her. A tone that never failed to soothe her when she doubted herself or was sad or even overjoyed. Today, it infused the finality of things. "May I come in?"

"Of course, Mother." Luci opened her eyes to see the marchioness take the brush from her maid and nod for Charlotte to depart. With a sigh, the older woman took over the lady's maid's chore, brushing Luci's thick, onyx hair from scalp to tip as she had when Luci was younger before it was deemed improper for a woman to spend so much time with her children as companions.

For the span of a heartbeat, she thought to

unburden the weight on her shoulders; throw herself at her mother's feet and beg she do something to right the situation.

However, her weak smile of greeting died on her lips.

Lady Camden never made eye contact with her eldest child but preferred to keep her stare on the brush in her hand. The action was all too unfamiliar for Luci. Even at meals, with all her children gathered, the marchioness did not speak to anyone beyond a comment on the weather or a question about the schoolroom. She'd given up her role as matriarch of the family many years ago, around the time her magnificent black hair had turned grey, seemingly overnight, and her deep green eyes had dulled, any spirit they'd once held vanishing with her last strands of self-respect.

She was a woman born into a world that afforded her no decisions beyond those allowed by her father—and later, her husband. Certainly, she was charged with planning the meals for the household, securing the proper clothing for the children, making sure they attended their studies and prepared for University. Beyond that, Luci knew the marchioness lived a solitary life; cut off from her family years prior with no friends to speak of now beyond her four children. And even they had become silent observers to their mother's pain.

All while the man she'd pledge to love and service was serving other women.

That was a fate worse than death for Luci.

No matter the fury inside her, Luci was incapable of changing the course of Lord and Lady Camden's marriage; however, she could never resent her mother for the life she'd chosen. Lady Camden's four children were well taken care of, educated, and would make fine matches—even if Luci's match was to a man over double her years.

"Mama," Luci sighed, her eyes drifting closed once more, desperately needing to be a child again, to go back to before her mother was broken—or maybe it was just before her children noticed how injured and beaten down she was.

"Yes, my fox." Her mother set the brush aside and stared into the dressing table mirror as Luci's eyes fluttered open.

Smiling, Luci said, "You haven't called me that in years."

"I haven't felt the need to remind you of your wit, your cunning, and your intelligence for some time." Her mother sighed, and she appeared far older, if not wiser, than her thirty-seven years. "You are able to see through deception and take swift action to change any situation. You are very brave, my fox."

"This may be beyond my control, Mama." Luci reached up and grasped her mother's hands that hovered directly over her shoulders. "I fear Father is not one to be trifled with, especially when he believes this match will benefit his many business ventures."

The marchioness clicked her teeth and shook her head. "I have long thought you would be the one to rescue us all from your father's domineering, cruel ways. Especially with your secretive activities since Tilda's death—"

"You know, Mama?" Suddenly, Luci had to see her mother's eyes, know if her mother detested Lucianna's means for handling the unsavory man in their lives.

"I was uncertain, at first, but then, after the night your father brought his mistress to that ball, well..." Her mother focused once more on her task of brushing Luci's hair. "When the *Gazette* soundly thumped your father, I knew you had had a hand in the deed. And while I said nothing, inwardly, I cheered your spirit and your bravery for calling out the man." She went silent for a moment, and Luci's heart skipped a beat. It was the first time, in many years, Luci felt she had an ally in her home instead of more people to protect. "You will save us all, I have no doubt."

It was much to ask of a mere slip of a girl, barely venturing into womanhood; however, Luci never wanted to let her mother down. She feared that if she did, the woman would lose all hope for her future and that of her younger offspring if left solely to the devices and whims of Lord Camden.

There was so much pressure in her mother's few words.

Lady Lucianna was to be her mother's only hope for survival.

Her chin lowered as she pondered the greatness her family expected of her. Anger raced up her spine to think everyone seemed to believe it was her responsibility to prove Abercorn had killed Tilda, to stop her father's overreaching abuse of his family, and to find a way to stop her betrothal to Abercorn.

She was only nineteen. She'd never been outside of England, and even more rarely away from London proper. How could anyone think her strong enough, witty enough, cunning enough, to do anything to help them—let alone drastically alter her own life's path.

"Mama," Luci asked, pressing her mother's hand to her cheek. "When did you decide to give up, allow Father the reins, and step back into the shadows?"

She knew from the tears brimming in her mother's eyes that she'd hurt her, but still, the question hung in the air. "I have never given up, Lucianna."

"But Father does whatever he wants. He parades around one mistress after another, rarely accompanies us to societal gatherings, and we hear him shouting at you when you think we are all fast asleep."

Luci watched as a small smile spread across her mother's face, making her appear not much older than Luci herself. "I think you have the wrong impression, my little fox."

"How?"

"He parades around his mistresses because I give him leave to. He decided early in our marriage he was not cut out to be the husband I desired, and so, he's lived all these years without me by his side."

"That is your choice?" Luci was shocked, stunned almost into silence. "Does it not hurt to see him showing off his mistresses?"

"At first, certainly." The marchioness sighed. "I thought, 'what have I done? I pushed my husband away because I could not bring myself to accept him for the man he is.' Over time, this did not concern me because I have always had the task of raising you and your siblings in proper fashion."

Luci doubted she knew her mother at all.

If one did not know their own flesh and blood, what would keep her from doubting every person she met and the society she'd been born into?

"Your brothers will grow to be kind, compassionate, humorous, loving, and loyal men. It is sad it took your father's disloyalty to his family to show Matthew and Derek all the things they did not want to be."

"What of Candace and me?" Luci asked. "Are we growing and learning in your image?"

"Heavens no, my child." The marchioness came around and sat next to Luci on the bench. "I have raised the pair of you to be independent. Taught you to make your own decisions. Never fear risk or the rewards that might come from it. Oh, and most importantly, I've taught you both to never allow a man like your father to dictate your life. Lucianna, use your cunning and your wit to take hold of your fate." She squeezed her daughter's hands.

"And what happens when I am gone?" Luci sighed. "You, Candace, and the boys will be alone against that monster."

Her mother's chuckle was infused with a deep hurt, driving Luci to apologize, but her mother held up her hand to silence her. "You cannot worry about us. Your brothers will leave for University before long, and

Candace still has many lessons to learn, but I will endeavor to keep her away from your father."

"And you?" Luci looked into her mother's deep green eyes, so much like hers though they held an exhaustion Luci hadn't noticed.

"I will continue as I always have, loving the man I married and praying every day he returns to the kind, honorable lord I was proud to wed all those years ago."

Had her mother had a plan all this time?

An ache settled deep in Luci's chest at the thought that her mother had known her goal all along but had not thought enough of her daughter to share. Luci could not believe that to be true.

"He is a horrible man, but you still love him." Luci leaned her cheek on her mother's shoulder. "That is—"

"The place that hope begins, draws strength."

"How can you be so certain he will return to the man you married?" Luci begged.

"I am certain of nothing except where my own heart lies. And that is with your father."

"Even if he does horrid things? Even when his temper gets the best of him? Even when he demands your daughter wed an unsavory, dishonorable man?"

"Just because the Marquis of Camden demands something does not mean it is to be."

A rattle at her terrace sounded, pulling Luci's attention from her mother to the windowpaned French doors leading onto her private veranda overlooking the street below.

"Did you hear that?" Luci asked.

Her mother tilted her head and listened, just as another round of rattling assaulted her panes.

She shook her head. "No, I am sorry. I do not hear a thing. However, I will request that Charlotte and the housekeeper allow you to rest. Someone will be by later this evening to stoke the fire."

The women stood and embraced. How long had it been since she'd set her arms around her mother and pulled her close? She'd half expected to find the older woman's shoulders gaunt and bony, as if she wasted away due to neglect, but her mother's shoulders were as solid as Luci remembered them.

Another handful of pebbles clattered along the veranda and hit the window.

"Are you certain you hear nothing?"

Her mother smirked before pecking Luci on the cheek and turning to leave. "Have a *restful* night, my little fox. Do not forget, a fox always knows their way, even in the dead of night."

Luci swore she heard her mother chuckle as she closed the door to her daughter's room.

Pushing her waist-length black hair over her shoulder, Luci hurried to the door and turned the lock before facing the unmistakable sound coming from her veranda.

Her heart thumped nearly out of her chest as another spray assaulted the window.

For only a brief moment, Luci considered fleeing her room and calling for a footman to explore where the noise had come from.

Even with that plan still solidly in mind, Luci moved toward the French doors and reached for the latch.

CHAPTER 17

RODERICK HUFFED, TOSSING yet another handful of pebbles toward the lit window above. His head pounded relentlessly following his meeting with Camden and Abercorn. His arm ached from throwing so many bloody rocks at Lady Lucianna's veranda. And blast it all, he was sick and tired of the pitying looks from Torrington, Lady Ophelia, and Lady Edith. To make matters worse—much, much worse—at some point, Torrington's younger sisters had joined the party.

Lady Chastity and Lady Prudence were agreeable enough young women; however, they talked a lot. They spoke of never having met Roderick before. They spoke of Lady Edith's grand ball. They chattered on about Lady Ophelia's new hairstyle.

The veranda they all stood on was large, yet the group's combined excitement seemed to reduce the area to that of a confined, closed carriage.

Giving Roderick little time to ponder his next move—and there had to be a next move, and fast. His blood boiled at the thought of the alternative…

Lord Camden had settled on the Duke of Abercorn as the best marriage prospect for Lucianna.

He hadn't even entertained any additional offer from Roderick.

Lucianna's fate had been secured and signed before Roderick could ask for a drink. His interest had all been for show, to push Abercorn to offer more and make more business agreements to have Lucianna as wife.

Bloody hell, but that was not the end of things.

Lucianna deserved far more than to be bartered like an old boat in jeopardy of capsizing due to her hellion tendencies and disagreeable nature.

She was not disagreeable, only adamant against the misdeeds of others.

She deserved to be cherished and loved. She deserved a home and a family of her own. She deserved to never fear the man she was wed to.

Roderick was unsure if he could give her everything she ought to have, but right now, at this moment, he was the best option for her.

"Mayhap if you aimed a bit higher, Your Grace," Ophelia said, mimicking her improved throwing style. "The pebbles are certain to hit the window then."

"What if she isn't in her room?" he asked, worried the auburn-haired nymph had used up her daily supply of words.

"Then Pru and I will go to the door and knock," Lady Chastity offered.

It struck Roderick as odd a woman he'd met less than an hour before would risk anything to help him gain a word with Lucianna.

"Shhhh," Edith swiped at the air. "I think I heard the latch unlock."

"Oh, the door is opening," Pru and Chastity said in unison, clapping their hands.

"Do quiet that noise." Torrington turned a scowl on his sisters, but it vanished quickly. "It might not be Lady Lucianna who steps out—and we will all need move quickly to hide."

"Who—who—who—" Lucianna's normally deep, confident tone echoed down from above. "Who is it?"

Roderick stepped from the shadows at the tree line

and into the pool of moonlight below her veranda. They'd arrived when it was still light outside, but the day had passed to twilight as they'd bided their time.

He despised hearing the fright in her tone.

"It is I, Lady Lucianna."

"The grim reaper!" At Luci's sharp inhale, Ophelia elbowed Edith, and the two fell into a fit of giggles.

"Montrose, Edith, Ophelia?" She moved farther onto the veranda to look over the edge and see them all standing below. "What in heaven's name are you all doing here?"

"We are here, too!" Lady Chastity chimed in, not one to be left out. "Pru and I."

"Again, what are you all doing here? My father deposited me at home and returned to the duke's residence. He should return shortly," she sighed. "He will find you."

"With luck, he will find none of us." Montrose moved around to the stone steps leading up to Lucianna's private veranda. He took the stairs two at a time and was standing before her in an instant.

She was gowned in a fine nightshift of pure white—all innocence, only broken by the waves of onyx hair that hung clear past her waist. Her toes peeked from beneath her night rail, blessedly bare. She was everything Roderick knew her to be—except her chin no longer tilted upward slightly, and her shoulders sagged.

"My lady," Montrose croaked. She was far more beautiful than he remembered, but he loathed her air of sorrow. "I am here."

"Shall I assume my father officially gave Abercorn leave to announce our betrothal?" Lucianna sobbed, a deep, heart-wrenching cry.

Every emotion from the long day drained from him at her cry; anger, fury, desperation, longing, and hurt—he could not grasp and hold onto a single one. His resolve shook, barely holding together.

"What your father says means naught to us," he soothed, running his hand down her back before pulling her close. "I have a plan—with the help of your friends."

"What? We will just run off to Gretna Green and be wed in disgrace?" She cringed at the word, knowing she'd brought the term down on his head. "My father will likely expect that move and send a group of servants to catch us before we reach the border."

"There are other ways." His mind swirled, trying to land on another option for them, but he could only think of Lucianna in his arms—and keeping her there. "We will find another way."

"Or mayhap it would be best to return to my chambers and await my father's decree that will solidify my future." She pulled away slightly as if to do just that.

But Roderick had her in his embrace, and it would take far more than the Marquis of Camden to take the woman he loved from him.

He stiffened.

The woman he loved?

Blast it all, but he *did* love her.

It had been many years since he'd experienced anything resembling love, and never a love like this. Yes, he'd loved and adored his mother. He'd respected and loved his father.

But never had he dreamt of loving a woman, especially a female as deserving of love as Lady Lucianna.

There would be no compromise. She belonged to him, as his heart belonged to her.

Never again would he allow her to entertain the notion that she might be forced to wed Abercorn.

"Lucianna, I love you," he said as he kissed her forehead.

"Love makes wise people do foolish things." She pulled back to look up at him.

Her eyes were clouded with confusion, yet

Roderick didn't feel confused at all. He set his hands against her cold cheeks. "And it makes a foolish person do wise things. Like finding the woman they love and holding on, no matter what consequences lay ahead."

"Can it be so simple?" she asked.

A shiver ran through her, and her teeth chattered.

Roderick hadn't thought about how chilled the evening had grown, especially with Lucianna gowned in nothing but a thin nightshift. "Let us return inside, and I will show you."

In her chambers, he would have all night to convince her that finding love and holding onto it was just that simple, as long as she felt the same.

But first, he needs must share with her the rest of his sordid past. She needed to know everything before she decided to thwart her father.

Even Roderick had enough integrity to discourage allowing a woman to fall in love with him until she knew the whole truth.

Taking her hand, Roderick turned toward her open veranda door and the warmth that certainly lay within. Surprisingly, she followed without resistance. If she hadn't, he'd been prepared to sweep her off her feet and carry her back to the heated bedchambers.

CHAPTER 18

LUCIANNA ALLOWED RODERICK to guide her back into her bedchambers as she walked on shaky legs. She still held out hope that her father cared about what she wanted for her own future, but when Roderick—with all her friends in tow—had shown up below her veranda, she more than suspected that her father had chosen Abercorn to be her husband.

She'd been mastered, conquered, and bested by the one man who should care most for her. To know the man she'd grown up trying to impress, the man Luci currently did her best to emulate, didn't care a whit for her...hurt. Her father didn't bother himself with grandiose thoughts of love, devotion, commitment, and friendship.

Her head spun when she lowered her chin to hide her feelings.

The Marquis of Camden did not have those things in his marriage, and so, he did not think it of value to his daughter.

Well, the marquis was gravely wrong.

Those were the qualities Luci searched for in not only her future husband but also her friends.

She and Roderick stood before her hearth, facing the flames, their fingers entwined; everything and everyone receding as she could only see him.

This was exactly how Luci saw herself with her husband: at peace, trusting one another, and forever entwined.

She wanted not only their fingers intertwined but also their minds, bodies, and souls.

So fused together people around them wondered how had they achieved such elevated love.

It would never be about one dominating the other—not with she and Roderick. Never would they make the other feel insignificant, unheard, or unwanted.

"Roderick," she gulped. When he looked down at her, his normally intense blue eyes were a meadow of blue blossoms, welcoming and inviting. "I am ready to see what simple looks like. Show me?"

He needed no other encouragement. Roderick swept her into his arms and crossed the room to her lilac fabric-covered bed and pushed aside the white, eyelet drapes.

The feeling of her of bed coverlet against her back had never been so soft or welcoming. In fact, she'd always seen the room as childish, but with Roderick's dark presence in the small space, the room took on an entirely new feel. The lilac and deep violet were exotic hues—begging for the couple's weight.

Roderick paused above her, fanning her dark hair out around her on the bed before pressing a kiss to the tip of her nose. "I have long wondered how beautiful you would be with your hair spread across my bed. I'll compromise for your bed, just this once."

"Your Grace!" Luci's cheeks heated at the meaning behind his words, only to flame further with his final words. He planned to take her to his bed soon. "What if someone enters my chambers?"

"Let them," he mumbled, placing tiny kisses along her cheek, down to her jaw, and over to her ear.

He was unafraid of the scene they'd cause if caught tonight in her chambers, and neither was she concerned.

Luci and her friends had spent years whispering about what happened behind closed bedchamber doors...and Roderick was the perfect—the only—man to show her, teach her.

Her body melted into the contours of the bed at the confidence in his words.

Roderick placed several kisses on her neck before pushing back and balancing on his hands above her.

"There is something I need to tell you before we continue," he sighed.

He was going to tell her he loved her again.

And by all that was holy, Luci would have to admit she loved him too or risk seeing him leave her and pull away for good.

And it would be what she deserved. To love someone meant to trust them implicitly. Luci wondered how long love could last when trust was unspoken...

"I am bankrupt, without funds beyond those necessary to keep my lands and tenants' homes out of disrepair." He lowered his head, their foreheads touching. "When my father died, I found out that he'd willingly given over all of my family's money to a corrupt gambling hell ring. No paperwork, no names, no way of finding what rightly belongs to me and mine."

She gasped, and he instantly pulled back further, sliding his body off hers to lie beside her.

Love was not about money or belongings.

It was about belonging to someone who loved you more than money.

The void above her made her long to cry out, demand he return and lay his body atop hers once more.

"And the woman at the opera?" It was Luci's one reservation about Roderick. He'd been more than clear and honest about Lady Daphne—he had no feelings for her, but what of the woman she'd spied him with that night months ago? "Do you love her?"

"Love her?" Roderick gave a deep, twisted chuckle, and Luci's chest seized.

Would she be able to accept his current words of love and put out of mind his past love?

"I told you, Lady Cavendish is my father's best friend's widow." He stared into her eyes intently. "She also lost everything when her husband died, and she found out he'd promised it all to this underground gambling hell, as well—including her widow's settlement. She had found a lead, and I was meeting with her to discover what she knew. The woman had no funds to hire a Bow Street runner to track down her inheritance, but, because I was fated to marry Lady Daphne and have use of her dowry, I figured I could investigate what she found further."

"And I ruined that for you…"

"No," he said, shaking his head and placing a kiss on her forehead to ease her frown. "You may have slowed me down and made it impossible to discover the lead Lady Cavendish discovered, but with Lucian's help, I have continued searching."

"You did not learn what she knew at the opera?"

"She was fearful of bringing the documentation she'd discovered to such a public place in case we were discovered. I was to meet with her the following day in a secluded area of Regent's Park."

"But the *Mayfair Confidential* article wrecked that plan?"

"Yes, Lady Cavendish did not show up for our appointment," he admitted. "Her townhouse is vacant. There is no one at her country estate. She has disappeared from society, just as she'd planned to do after she gave me the information I needed." Roderick sighed, averting his eyes and taking in the room for the first time. "I suppose Abercorn is not looking all too unsuitable now, huh?"

"Even if we were made to live on the streets of London, and I was forced to push an orange cart outside Vauxhall, I would still favor you over Lord Abercorn." Lucianna pushed from her back and slung her leg over Roderick, forcing him to lay flat. "There are many things in this world I question, but that, I do not."

It was her turn to lean down, halting an inch before their lips touched. "I am eternally sorry." She placed a kiss against his lips when he tried to silence her. "There is not a day I would choose another."

"Even if your father demands it?" he asked hesitantly.

Was he scared of what her answer would be?

Suddenly, Luci was terrified to say the words because once said, she could not take them back. Her course would be set. Although, her path had been unalterable since she'd bested Roderick at Bentley's only several days earlier.

So little time had passed, yet everything had changed for her. She'd never thought to wed after what Tilda had gone through. Yes, a spark of hope had started when Edith met Torrington and fell madly and deeply in love, but that spark had turned to a flame when Luci had stumbled upon Roderick. Even now, it pooled in her belly—and lower—growing with intensity by the minute as she stared down into the eyes of the man she'd never dreamt of loving.

With her hair falling on both sides of his face, she bent down and placed her lips to his. There was no better way to give her answer than to show him.

Luci had no need to fight for control where Roderick was concerned. He allowed her to explore at her leisure, her lips trailing across his cheek and to his neck; however, she kept going until her mouth met his ear. She flicked her tongue out and drew the lobe between her lips, gently sucking.

Tendrils of need coursed through her, and she released his flesh.

His whimper told her he wanted her to continue, but she had many other places to explore. Sights she'd never seen.

Roderick's hands caressed her backside, traveling

lower to rest on her rounded bottom. The feel of his strong hands through her nightshift was unmistakable. The heat coursing through the thin fabric warmed her.

Gently, she rotated her hips and rubbed against the flap of his trousers, surprised at his manhood's hardening. The desire rolling through her had Luci pulling back and sitting straight, enabling her to push her most delicate place closer to his hard length.

She was the hellion she'd always been accused of being, but this—everything about her and Roderick— was right. Her pulse fluttered with her weakness for him, at the same moment her heart soared with empowerment.

His hands left her backside, caressing up her sides to cup her breasts, his thumbs circling her nipples through her shift. He set a slow pace as he stared up at her, and his movements sent her heart thundering as she continued to move against him.

Her yearning intensified until Luci feared she would burst into flames and perish from desire, taking Roderick with her.

"You are beautiful, Lucianna," he mumbled as if drunk off the sight of her above him.

And he never took his stare from hers as his hands halted and he drew down the front of her shift, exposing her breasts.

For the measure of a heartbeat, she moved to cover herself, but he stopped her when he took hold of her hands, placing them on his chest. She couldn't keep them still as she massaged the muscles along his chest and shoulders, sculpted from years holding a foil.

His breath hitched as she untied his cravat and moved to unbutton his shirt and expose him as much as she was visible to him.

Finally, she spread his shirt wide and smoothed her hands over his chest, sprinkled with fine, black hair. Luci shouldn't be shocked by the striking look of her white hands moving across his tanned skin. The contrast was erotic, and Luci was helpless to look away. His skin was as smooth and unblemished as her hands. His tan led down his chest…disappearing into his waistband.

How did the sun's rays touch every inch of his body?

She almost asked, but Roderick shifted below her, pushing up onto his elbows.

She flung her head back when he took her hardened nipple into his mouth, his tongue playing in circles, mimicking the motion she'd inflicted on his earlobe.

Ecstasy.

Pure, scorching hot desire flowed from her head to her toes.

Her core pulsed, demanding no clothes separate them, their bodies needing to be skin to skin.

"What is the bloody meaning of this?" her father's voice thundered, bouncing off her walls and rattling the windowpanes at the same time the latch burst on her door. "Lucianna, what have you done?"

Roderick pulled back, releasing her nipple and returning her shift to cover her exposed breasts.

"Father…I…" She fumbled to refasten the buttons on Roderick's shirt, but her fingers shook, and he pushed her hands away. Thankfully, her long, black hair shielded them from sight. "Do give us a moment."

"Give you a moment?" The marquis fumed. Luci heard rather than saw him stalk into the room. Roderick lifted her from him and set her on the side of the bed before finishing with his shirt. "So you can continue to sully what is mine? In this ruined state, you are worthless to me. I fear I will have to pay—and pay handsomely—just to be rid of you."

Luci realized her father thought her utterly compromised and beyond saving.

She opened her mouth to correct him but clamped it shut again, not bothering to hide her grin.

CHAPTER 19

RODERICK STARED INTO Lucianna's face, expecting all color to drain as panic set in…instead, a coy grin had settled on her, and her shoulders straightened as she scooted to the edge of the bed and stood.

The pristine white nightshift billowed around her legs, covering her naked calves and teasing her bare feet.

The tilt of her chin and narrowed stare had Roderick thinking she was almost happy to face her father's rage. Brushing her long hair over her shoulder, she slowly walked across the room toward her father.

When Roderick sensed his desire had subsided enough, he moved from her bed and trailed in her wake until he stood directly behind her. He set his hands on both of her shoulders.

"Lord Camd—"

She held up her hand, cutting off his words.

He watched Camden's face redden, and his nostrils flare in anger, his hands clenched into fists at his sides. The man had every right to be furious, but not with Lucianna. If retribution were owed, it would be claimed from Roderick.

Roderick had been in the wrong. He'd known his course when he entered Lucianna's bedchambers, though he never would have acknowledged it before.

"Father." Her tone was laced with steel and conviction, as still and confident as the set of her shoulders. "You are too late. I am ruined. Solidly, unequivocally tarnished."

Her chin only lifted farther when Camden narrowed his stare on her. "You have been trouble since the day your mother gave birth to you. I always imagined you doing something foolish to scandalize this family."

Camden shook his head, feigning sympathy for Lucianna.

Roderick wanted to curse the man, tell him his daughter had lost nothing being caught in his embrace. If anything, she'd gained the world.

His world and everything he possessed.

Which wasn't much, but his love was worth more than riches.

"You will leave this house immediately. You have brought disgrace upon your mother, your siblings, and me." Camden pivoted and started toward the door, halting before he crossed the threshold. "And, Montrose, you can see your way out the same way you got in."

Without another word, the marquis stepped into the hall and shouted for the family butler.

A shiver ran down Lucianna's spine, and Roderick stilled himself from wrapping her in his arms, dispelling the chill that had settled along her arms.

Lucianna turned toward him, her shoulders stooping and tears threatening to fall.

Remorse weakened him for his part in her ruination.

"McMahon!" the marquis shouted as hurried footsteps sounded down the hall outside Lucianna's bedchambers. "See that my daughter leaves this house at once. She is to take nothing but a jacket to hide her damaged person."

"Yes, my lord." Reluctance was clear in the servant's voice.

"I will fix this, Lucianna. I swear to it." He stared down at her as she brushed away her unshed tears.

"There is nothing to fix." She shook her head, leaning into him. "This is what I wanted, exactly what I'd hoped for."

"But, your father…" Roderick sputtered, attempting to understand what she meant about it being exactly what she'd hoped for. "You've been cast out by your father…with nothing."

"I will stay with either Edith's or Ophelia's family. Do not fret," she said flatly.

"And what of your things?"

"They are just that, things." She turned a lopsided smile up to him, her cheek never leaving his chest. "But the one thing I will never have to deal with is Abercorn. He would never take a ruined woman to wife. No matter how large her dowry."

The woman, *his* woman, was a smart one.

Roderick had dwelled on all Lucianna was losing…and not on what she'd gain from a tarnished reputation.

"But how will he know of your ruination?" he asked.

"You do not know my father very well, do you?" Her brow rose. "He does not take kindly to parting with his money. If he shuns me publicly, he will remain in possession of my dowry."

"And not have to put up with your hellion ways."

"Correct, Your Grace." She pulled away from him and placed a kiss on his cheek. "You are certainly catching on."

"Yes, it is a positive thing that I am no dullard…and I happen to adore your hellion ways."

"Do you?" she asked with a deep, throaty laugh.

"Oh, yes." He pulled her against his chest. "I do believe your misfortune is to be my grand blessing."

"Did he call her a blessing?" A hiss sounded behind him.

"No, I think he called her depressing," Lord Torrington's unmistakable tone could be heard from the open veranda door.

"Why would he call her depressing?" Lady Edith chimed in. "I do believe he is instructing her in her undressing."

A round of female giggles echoed as the group all but fell into Lucianna's chambers.

"Tell us, Montrose," Torrington called, pulling Edith to his side. "Is Lady Lucianna a blessing, depressing, or in need of undressing?"

"You all have magnificent timing." Roderick leaned down and placed a kiss to Lucianna's forehead, which gained a sigh from Lady Prudence and Lady Chastity, while Lady Ophelia looked ready to faint on the spot. "I was actually professing my adoration and love for Lady Lucianna and hoping our night would end with her acquiescing and accepting my marriage proposal."

"Marriage?" Lucianna squeaked. "But we just thwarted my father's plans to hand me over to Abercorn…there is no need for you to continue your charade and our sham of a betrothal. I will not be responsible for you taking on a dismal future and a bride you never wanted."

"That is wonderful news; however, I have never been one for charades, nor one for 'taking on a dismal future and a bride.' I've longed to have you since that early morning at Bentley's. That did not change after our meeting in the gardens at Lady Edith's betrothal ball."

The women sighed again, but Lucianna flinched back with a frown.

"Lady Lucianna, I love you. I am in love with you." Roderick released her and brought his hands to cradle her face. "I do not care if you come to me with little more than your nightshift. I will live every day showering you with all the possessions your heart desires."

Her bottom lip trembled, and Roderick's breath hitched, thinking she'd turn away from him. He was no more than a poverty-stricken duke, while she'd been raised by one of the wealthiest men in all of England.

"My heart desires only you, Roderick."

He pulled her close, fearing she'd never be near enough to satisfy him, and doubting he'd ever be able to let her out of his sight.

"Say you will marry me, Lucianna," he pleaded. He needed to hear her say it in front of all these witnesses. It would make everything real.

"Roderick, seventh Duke of Montrose, I, Lady Lucianna Constantine, love you," she declared loudly. "I will wed you and be a fierce duchess, the likes of which London has never seen before."

A cheer went up behind him as he crushed Lucianna to him, no longer caring who witnessed their display of affection for one another.

All of London best prepare; the Duke and Duchess of Montrose were sure to leave a trail of fainting matrons and fawning men in their wakes.

EPILOGUE

LUCIANNA WALKED ARM in arm with Ophelia from the bedchambers they'd shared since the marquis had cast her from her home. Never in her life had she felt the depth of contentment she did since being thrown out of her family home without a shilling to her name and agreeing to wed Roderick.

The Duke and Duchess of Atholl, Ophelia's parents, had gladly taken Luci in and given her a place to stay until she and Roderick were properly wed, affording the couple a much-needed air of propriety.

The girls took the stairs two at a time, each holding tightly to the railing.

Roderick should arrive at any moment to collect them for their late-morning shopping excursion to Bond Street. It had been over a fortnight, and Luci had grown tired of letting the hems out on Ophelia's gowns—and having to see her friend's scathing looks each time she noticed another of her gowns gone.

When an envelope arrived for her the night before, Luci had worried her father was demanding she return home and insisting she fulfill his wishes to wed Abercorn; however, the paper held her mother's elegant script, and inside, was a note for one thousand pounds. Not nearly enough to secure a favorable future for her and Roderick, but a more than adequate amount to afford her a shopping trip and to pay a Bow Street runner to track down Lady Cavendish and the men who'd stolen from Roderick's father.

That was, if Roderick allowed her to spend her funds helping him.

There was also Abercorn to think of. Would it be possible to hire the same runner to keep watch on the duke? They'd all determined it was not wise—or safe— to spy on the man themselves any longer. However, Luci had come close to being wed to the man. Another woman would fall into his trap sooner rather than later…and they had a duty to prevent that from occurring.

Luci's mother's letter went on to express her well wishes for the betrothed couple and contained a promise to see Luci's father released her remaining dowry upon her wedding day. Luci had little hope that the marquis would ever acquiesce where money was concerned. She only dreaded her father taking his anger out on her mother and siblings.

A loud knock sounded at the door as Ophelia and Luci took their overcoats from the footman.

"Lord Montrose is certainly a punctual gent," Ophelia mumbled, glancing at the tall clock in the hall.

Ten-thirty sharp.

Not a moment early, and not a second late.

The butler scurried from his pantry to greet their guest, but when he opened the door, it was not Roderick's dark-haired form waiting on the stoop, but a man with hair of pure spun gold.

"Who is that?" Luci leaned in and whispered to Ophelia. "If I were not deeply smitten with Roderick, I think I would find this man very handsome."

Ophelia put her finger to her lips to shush her friend and stepped back into the stairwell and out of sight. Lucianna followed Ophelia's lead as the butler ushered the man toward Ophelia's father's study.

"I haven't the vaguest idea who he is." Ophelia leaned forward, catching a glimpse of the man's back as he entered the study. The door closed behind him, just as another knock sounded at the door.

"That must be Roderick." She leapt from the stairwell and hurried into the foyer as the butler returned to answer the door, but when she glanced over her shoulder, Ophelia hadn't followed.

She stood still, staring at her father's study.

"Good morn, ladies." Roderick stepped over the threshold. "You both look fine today. Are we ready for an exhaustive day of shopping?"

"Hello, Your Grace," Luci called, stepping into her betrothed's open arms. "I can say I have thought of nothing else since my mother's note arrived."

He placed a quick peck on her cheek. "And I am certain Lady Ophelia has grown tired of you ruining her gowns."

Lucianna laughed, turning to Ophelia, but she'd moved in the direction of her father's study.

"Are you coming?" Luci called to her friend's retreating back.

Ophelia waved over her shoulder. "I think I will remain home," she said over her shoulder. "Edith and Lord Torrington will be meeting you, correct?"

"Yes, but—"

"No one likes a fifth wheel, as they say."

Roderick shrugged, and Luci turned back to see her friend press her ear to her father's door.

"Shall we be off?" Roderick took Luci's gloved hand and set it on his arm. "I believe she is duly occupied, and we have a bridal *trousseau* to gather before we depart for Scotland."

Luci nodded, her mind already swirling around the notion of her and Roderick being properly wed and free to live as husband and wife. They'd leave for Gretna Green in two days' time, with Edith and Lord Torrington, as well as Lady Prudence and Lady Chastity, coming as their witnesses.

Ophelia would stay behind, being an unmarried maiden; her mother forbidding her travel to Scotland.

"Are you having second thoughts?" Roderick whispered, his mouth a scant hair's breadth from her ear. "Because, if you are, I can always cancel—"

Luci swatted at him as they started out the door. "Of course, I am not having any second thoughts. However, I was thinking a great deal of you laid across my bed, your shirt undone, and me atop you."

"You minx," he said with a chuckle. "Though I would be less than honest if I didn't admit I have thought of the same thing nonstop for the last fortnight. Do you think after we are wed your father will allow us entry to your old bedchambers?"

Lucianna winked as he handed her into his coach. "No need to ask permission. I learned long ago that the lock on the veranda door is rather easy to dislodge."

"Heaven help us if our children are blessed with your cunning and smarts." He entered the coach after her, and Luci used that moment to spring onto his lap, straddling his legs with her thighs on each side.

She gave him her most practiced coquettish smile and batted her eyelashes for good measure. "Bond Street is at least a ten-minute drive with morning traffic."

"You hellion, we will be lucky to make it to Scotland!" Roderick said with a chuckle before leaning forward to capture her lips.

"And I'm sure that won't be a hardship, Your Grace," she said with a wink as she pulled back.

"I love you, Luci. It may have taken my misfortune to bring us together, but having you in my life makes me the richest man alive."

AUTHOR'S NOTES

Thank you for reading *The Misfortune of Lady Lucianna
(The Undaunted Debutantes, Book Two)*.

If you enjoyed *The Misfortune of Lady Lucianna*,
be sure to write a brief review at any retailer.

I'd love to hear from you!

You can contact me at:
Christina@christinamcknight.com

Or write me at:
P.O. Box 1017
Patterson, CA 95363

www.ChristinaMcKnight.com
Check out my website for giveaways, book reviews, and
information on my upcoming projects,
or connect with me through social media at:

Twitter: @CMcKnightWriter
Facebook: www.facebook.com/christinamcknightwriter
Goodreads: www.goodreads.com/ChristinaMcKnight

Sign up for my newsletter here:
http://eepurl.com/VP1rP

**For more information about
The Undaunted Debutantes, turn the page!**

THE UNDAUNTED DEBUTANTES

Three innocent debutantes must work to solve the mysterious death of their childhood friend. With undaunted determination they pledge to not only expose the man responsible for their friend's tragic death on her wedding night, but to also uncover other unscrupulous men of the *ton* who would jeopardize the future of other young women.

The Disappearance of Lady Edith
The Misfortune of Lady Lucianna
The Misadventures of Lady Ophelia

AVAILABLE IN PRINT AND E-BOOK

The Disappearance of Lady Edith
Book 1
Available May 23, 2017

One tragic night changed sensible, proper Lady Edith Pelton's life: when her best friend fell to her death, pushed down a flight of stairs by a nefarious lord. Now, Edith dedicates her time to watching the man she thinks is responsible, while gathering information to expose other scoundrels posing as gentlemen of honor about London. When her spying is noticed by a perfect stranger, Edith finds herself with two mysteries—what happened to her friend, and how to win the heart of this brilliantly handsome lord.

The Misadventures of Lady Ophelia
Book 3
Available July 11, 2017

If only Lady Ophelia Fletcher—quiet, reserved, with her nose always stuck in a book—had witnessed the death of her friend that fateful night. Desperate to make amends for holding her tongue the night her dear friend was murdered, she now she writes a column, *Mayfair Confidential,* that she uses to expose men with unsavory pasts. But when a handsome stranger arrives to meet with her father, Ophelia can't help but do a little investigating for her own benefit. At last, she's stumbled upon an adventure of her own—but does she possess the skills necessary to solve the mystery without the assistance of her friends?

**See how it all starts for
The Undaunted Debutantes in this excerpt from
*The Disappearance of Lady Edith!***

AN EXCERPT FROM
THE DISAPPEARANCE OF LADY EDITH

It is hereby stated that this writer has born firsthand witness to the 7th Duke of Montrose, scandalously alone with a golden-haired nymph in his private opera box, all whilst betrothed to the widow, Lady Cavendish.

As this writer can also attest, Lady Cavendish's hair is pure night, compared to the observed doxy's crown of light. Let this article stand as proof that Lady Cavendish would do well to find herself another eligible lord to take as husband.

-*Mayfair Confidential, London Daily Gazette*

St. James Place, London
January 1815

TRISTON NEVILLE, VISCOUNT Torrington, glared at his father, forcing himself to breathe in deeply and hold the stale air, heavy with cigar smoke, in his lungs to avoid it exiting in a rush of rage.

The Marquis of Downshire couldn't possibly fathom what he was asking of his son. Triston doubted his father understood the ludicrous nature of his demands, masked as simple fatherly requests.

"Did you hear me, Triston?" His father's nostrils flared, and the tiny vein that ran up his forehead pulsed...once, twice, three times. The man's frown deepened, and Triston was uncertain if the marquis was annoyed at his son's antics or only mildly agitated.

To be fair, Triston had been aiming for annoyance.

He straightened his shoulders, holding in his sigh once again, but responded before his father fainted from holding his breath. "Yes, Father. I heard you and will keep all you've said in mind."

"You will accompany your sisters during their Season?"

"Yes."

"You will endeavor to not draw attention to yourself and, therefore, away from your sisters?"

Triston looked up at the study ceiling, attempting to suppress his irritation. "I have never sought the *ton*'s notice, if you will remember."

Downshire stood, pushing his chair back. He placed his hand flat upon the desk separating the men and leaned forward. "That is neither here nor there."

In his younger days, Triston would have needed to steel himself from quaking in terror at his father's imposing stance and razor-edged words. However, those days passed when Triston grew several inches taller than the marquis, and his shoulders spread far wider than his sire's. Though both men towered over six feet in height and had matching golden-brown hair, Triston was larger on every scale that mattered—including intellect, which he hadn't vocalized since leaving the schoolroom for Eton.

"Father, I will do my best to make certain Lady Dow—" A movement over his father's shoulder, out the study window, caught Triston's notice. A flash of white was visible in the tree between the Downshire townhouse and their neighbor's. "I will make sure Esmee is not inconvenienced in any way."

Normally, his stepmother's name would have stuck in his throat, clawing to get free as he attempted to keep it unsaid. At present, he was determined not to allow the woman to overshadow his day; it was enough Triston would be forced to accompany the dreadful woman on social outings whenever she chose to attend.

His father nodded, apparently accepting Triston's pledge to see his sisters, Prudence and Chastity, safely wed before the year was out. To do that, the girls needed proper gowns with all the trimmings, and then needs must be presented to society to have the opportunity to meet eligible lords—all without their raven-haired stepmother criticizing their every move.

Triston leaned forward slightly to gain a better view out his father's study window. There was certainly something going on; however, alerting the marquis to it would not be wise and only lengthen their meeting. Blond hair hung down the back of a petite, female frame, the flash of her white petticoats being what had drawn his attention in the first place.

"Very well, Triston, I believe…" His father's brow scrunched, his eyes narrowing on his only son. "Are you even listening to me?"

"Of course." Triston took his eyes on the figure nestled in the tree. "It is only I have a prior engagement I am tardy for."

"A prior engagement, you say?" the marquis asked. His father's face reddened once more when Triston nodded. "You knew full well we meet each week at this precise time and place."

"Unfortunately, this could not be avoided." Triston shook his head as if he were loath to depart his father's home. "I surely must take my leave."

"If you must—"

Triston didn't wait for him to finish before turning and stalking toward the open study door.

His father's words echoed in his wake. "Impertinent, always were and always will be. Shut my door!"

Triston pulled the door closed, the thud reverberating through his entire body, though in a satisfying way.

He'd bought himself another week. Seven full days until he would be summoned again to his father's study to discuss trivial matters to keep up the appearance that the men were not at extreme odds with one another.

Triston only hoped that society had bought the ruse they'd been carrying on with since the marquis married his third and latest wife. If not, the *ton* would take great exception to his return to society, even with his two young sisters on his arms.

The hall window afforded a view similar to the study.

Triston took the few steps necessary and stood framed in the arched panes, gazing out as the afternoon sun warmed him through the glass. Sure enough, there was a woman perched in a Downshire tree, hunched over and staring at Lord Abercorn's upper window. A thick limb prodding her back prevented her from sitting completely upright.

It appeared his father requesting he accompany his sisters during their debut Season was only one of the peculiar occurrences he would witness during his day. Triston was hard-pressed to determine which was more alarming: his need to return to society, or a woman perched precariously in a plum tree.

Certainly, one did not regularly see a person, a woman especially, balanced on a thin tree limb at least six feet off the ground.

He tapped the window to gain her attention.

No response.

Triston looked up at the window she stared at, but the sun only reflected a glare off the glass, preventing him from seeing what held her attention.

Turning his focus toward the front drive and then back toward the gardens, Triston searched for the Downshire's groundskeeper. Frederick was usually tending the roses lining the drive during Triston's weekly visits to his father's home, but today he seemed to be absent.

He watched as the woman slipped something into her skirts, rubbing her hands together and looking about.

Was she not concerned someone would question why she was in a tree?

Triston shook his head. If the groundskeeper were

nowhere in sight, it was his responsibility to inquire as to why the woman was trespassing on Downshire property.

That and assist her down from her perilous post.

LADY EDITH PELTON sat perched in a tree, her head bent low, and a branch poking into her backside. She was filthy, she was sore, and she hadn't managed to learn anything from the last several hours. The only thing she'd witnessed was the duke moving from his office on the first floor to the second floor—after a particularly buxom woman with midnight locks had joined him. They hadn't entered any of the rooms facing her direction, nor had they returned below. That had been nearly an hour ago, and Edith had yet to note any other movement on the second floor, besides the occasional servant attending to their chores.

If she returned yet again with no new information on the Duke of Abercorn, nothing that condemned him for his wrongdoings—nor absolved him of his accused crimes—Lucianna would be irate. She'd likely demand to investigate the man herself, or worse yet, instruct Ophelia to write the article for the *Gazette*, attacking Abercorn, regardless of his culpability in Tilda's death.

Edith would not allow that to happen, could not permit her dear friend to ruin a man's life with no proof of his misconducts. Lucianna had agreed to wait until sufficient evidence existed, but with each passing day—and more articles submitted to the *Gazette*—her friend grew impatient.

Suddenly, a drapery on the second story toward the back of the townhouse was pulled aside, revealing a quite naked, raven-haired woman, her long tresses the only thing covering her exposed bosom.

It was impossible for Edith to take her eyes off the sight before her as the duke, fully clothed, stepped up behind the woman, wrapping his arms around her tightly as he fondled her breasts. The large window framed the couple perfectly. The woman began to sway before Abercorn, her backside still flush with his front.

Edith's face flamed red with embarrassment at the scandalous spectacle.

The duke whipped the woman around until her naked breasts were pressed against his chest, and the woman's rounded derriere pressed solidly against the windowpane. Abercorn slowly moved his lips to the woman's neck and traced his mouth along her shoulder before suddenly straightening and throwing his head back in a silent chuckle.

She wondered what the raven-haired beauty had said to gain such a reaction from the cold, stoic duke.

Edith's stare narrowed on the pair as the woman reached up and began to undo Abercorn's cravat.

Before Edith even suspected what was happening, the duke's eyes scanned the landscape outside his townhouse, his glare seeming to find Edith perched in the tree bordering his property. Abruptly, Edith ducked her head and slipped her journal into the secret pocket she'd sewn into each of her gowns for exactly this purpose before easing from the branch she sat on to scurry down the tree.

I cannot be caught, I cannot be caught, I cannot be caught, she chanted, placing her booted feet on another branch before dipping low to take hold of it and swing down to the ground below.

Almost there. Edith's hands were mere inches from grasping the thick limb to lower herself...only six feet from escape.

"You, there!" a deep voice sounded behind her. "What are you doing up there?"

"Eeep!" The sudden exclamation took her mind off the limb she reached for, and Edith's boot caught on her skirt, causing her to miss the branch completely. She stiffened her body as she fell, bracing for the impact she knew was to come as the air rushed by her.

The seconds slowed.

Giving her ample time to contemplate what she'd done in her life to end up falling from a tree in the fashionable St. James area of London, her arms pinwheeling as she hoped to ease her landing.

Thump.

Everything went dark, and Edith feared she'd landed on her head, doing irreparable damage.

She blinked several times and willed her mind to command her fingers to wiggle and her toes to curl in her boots.

Everything worked.

She said a silent prayer to whoever was looking out for her.

"I asked what you are doing on my property!" the man huffed.

Edith blinked again—still complete darkness. Maybe she *had* hit her head on the way down, but would it not ache?

"Do stop this ridiculousness and remove your garments from your head."

She moved silently, rolling to her side, a resounding pain in her backside cluing her in to exactly how she'd landed.

Lifting her hands, Edith pushed at whatever covered her sight, only to see a pair of Hessians solidly placed beside her. Lowering the material farther, she noted thick, muscular calves leading to tree trunk-sized thighs clad in tightly tailored breeches.

Edith cringed, allowing the material to fall back into place, blocking out all view of the man once more.

"I would suggest righting your skirts, as your derriere is exposed to all and sundry who happen to pass by on the street," the man commanded sternly.

From the dampness seeping from the ground beneath her hip and into her exposed knickers, Edith suspected she'd landed in a particularly well-tended and watered part of foliage.

The mention of her derriere brought back images of the raven-haired beauty's bare buttocks pressed firmly to the window of Abercorn's townhouse. Her face heated immediately, and Edith longed for nothing more than to stay hidden.

She wished a carriage would come along and put her out of her misery, as it were.

It was difficult to decide which was more embarrassing: her fall from the tree, her skirts being cast over her head, or that whoever the man standing above her was had witnessed it all.

"If I remain as such, will you go away and act as if this never happened?" Edith asked.

"What sort of gentleman would I be if I did not verify a damsel in distress was uninjured after a fall such as this?" His Hessians crunched dry, fallen leaves as he moved before her. "Besides, you are still trespassing, and I cannot allow that to go unresolved."

Suddenly, her skirts were pulled away, and Edith looked up, the bright sun momentarily blinding her, causing spots of colors to cross her vision. She closed her eyes tightly and rubbed at her face.

"I am going nowhere, so it's best if you remove your hands from your face and permit me to help you regain your feet."

"What if I simply roll myself into the street and allow the next carriage or man on horseback to resolve this dilemma for us?" she said into the palms of her gloved hands.

"I would say that is a mess I would not relish cleaning up." His stern tone had lessened, taking on an almost jovial quality.

Edith allowed her hands to fall from her face, and the man's outstretched hand appeared before her. She took a moment to ponder his offer, knowing if she raised her eyes to his, she'd be far more exposed than her backside had been only a moment before.

"Come now, I do not bite—unless commanded to," he said with a chuckle.

She couldn't avoid the man any longer. He was not going away, nor did he appear the type to allow questions to go unanswered.

But blast it all, Edith did not need to accept his assistance to gain her footing.

Her backside and pride were already bruised; she had no intentions of accepting his hand.

With a huff, Edith placed her gloved palms upon the dirt on either side of her, preparing to push herself to her feet—without his help.

But with the action, her gaze traveled from the man's offered hand and back to his thick thighs. The male could be a Highlander of old with such a foundation. Edith was helpless to stop her eyes from straying farther upward. His muscular legs gave way to a solid midsection that had her halting at his expansive chest. She need not allow her mind to wander far to know that under his linen shirt lay a chest of pure muscle, capped off by broad, sinewy shoulders certainly capable of lifting a fallen tree. Or a damsel in distress, as he'd dubbed her.

Edith swallowed, gulping down her purr of pleasure. What had overtaken her? He was only a man—a very *strong* man, his frame proving he exerted himself vigorously with regularity. It would not surprise her if he spent each day undertaking pursuits of manual labor, carrying carriage wheels as if they weighed no more than a bowl of orange marmalade.

He cleared his throat. "It is improper to stare, miss."

Edith's eyes widened in alarm. She *was* staring, and with no sense of regret. Whatever had come over her?

The moment she pushed on her palms to try and raise herself, a shot of pain traveled to her elbow. "Mayhap it is more than my backside that is bruised," she mumbled.

"I am here to assist," he repeated.

"You would like that much, I am certain, Lord—" Edith's words ended abruptly. She hadn't any notion if the man before her *was* a lord. He could be no more than a common gentleman. "I can stand without help, but thank you nonetheless."

"Torrington."

"Pardon?" Her eyes snapped to his face—another colossal mistake as her mouth gaped at the Adonis before her, the noonday sun highlighting his umber brown hair, chiseled jawline, and decidedly aristocratic nose. He was what the great poets of old wrote about in their sonnets. He was the image every artist struggled to achieve in oils. He was what sculptors in Roman times worked a lifetime to create.

And he was standing before her…flesh and blood.

His eyes seemingly capable of seeing to her very soul.

"My name, miss. Lord Torrington—Triston if you prefer, as I feel we are now adequately acquainted." He smirked at his jest and shook his hand before her face once more.

"Lord Torrington, it is," Edith said, relenting and taking his hand.

"Come, miss, we can do away with formalities. After all, I know the fabric of your knickers." His arrogant, amused grin grew, softening the hard line of his jaw—if it were possible.

At her gasp, he chuckled, hoisting her to her feet with one swift tug of her arm.

Available in print and e-book on May 23, 2017!

ABOUT THE AUTHOR

USA TODAY Bestselling Author Christina McKnight writes emotional and intricate Regency Romance with strong women and maverick heroes.

Her books combine romance and mystery, exploring themes of redemption and forgiveness. When she's not writing, Christina enjoys trying new coffeehouses, visiting wine bars, traveling the world, and watching television.

Email: Christina@ChristinaMcKnight.com
Follow her on Twitter: @CMcKnightWriter
Keep up to date on her releases:
www.christinamcknight.com
Like Christina's FB Author page:
ChristinaMcKnightWriter